GHOSTS of WAR
Fallen in Fredericksburg

Other Ghosts of War books

The Secret of Midway

Lost at Khe Sanh

AWOL in North Africa

Fallen in Fredericksburg

GHOSTS of WAR
Fallen in Fredericksburg

STEVE WATKINS

SCHOLASTIC INC.

All rights reserved. Published by Scholastic Inc., *Publishers since 1920*. SCHOLASTIC and associated logos are trademarks and/or registered trademarks of Scholastic Inc.

The publisher does not have any control over and does not assume any responsibility for author or third-party websites or their content.

This book is a work of fiction. Names, characters, places, and incidents are either the product of the author's imagination or are used fictitiously, and any resemblance to actual persons, living or dead, business establishments, events, or locales is entirely coincidental.

ISBN 978-0-545-83707-1

10 9 8 7 6 5 4 3 2 1   16 17 18 19 20

Printed in the U.S.A.   40
First printing 2016
Book design by Yaffa Jaskoll

For my mom, whose spirit will
always be close by

Greg Troutman, Julie Kobayashi, and I were totally killing it during band practice one afternoon the first week of December, down in the basement of my uncle's junk store. And by killing it, I mean we were really crushing it. And by really crushing it, I mean Greg and I had managed to tune our guitars pretty close to the way they're supposed to be tuned, and I was mostly keeping up on rhythm guitar with the tempo that Julie set on keyboards, and Greg was mostly hitting the right notes on his guitar solo, and I'd been able to mostly stay in tenor when I sang, though my voice kept straining to jump back up into boy-soprano range.

Boy soprano is the same as girl soprano except that I'm not a girl and it kind of seems important to make that distinction.

Anyway, we were killing it *and* crushing it, but then dogs started barking — a lot of dogs, the really loud kind. So loud that pretty soon we could barely hear ourselves playing.

Greg stopped first. "Oh man. Just when we were sounding good."

"Yeah," I said, or shouted. "Really good."

Julie kept playing but she was the only one, so in a minute she quit, too. "What did you say?" she shouted. "I can't hear because of the dogs!"

There weren't any dogs where we were, of course — in our basement practice room in this really old building in downtown Fredericksburg, Virginia. The barking was coming from next door at a place called Dog and Suds, a dog-grooming business that shared a wall with the Kitchen Sink. We'd sometimes heard them before, but never this loud.

"Come on!" I shouted. "Let's go upstairs and see what's going on over there. Maybe Uncle Dex can tell us something."

"What?" Julie shouted again. I figured she must have gone temporarily deaf, so I hand-signaled what we were doing. She turned off her keyboard and followed us, hands pressed over her ears.

It wasn't much quieter upstairs, but at least we could hear ourselves when we spoke. Uncle Dex, too. "Guess those dogs next door finally had enough of your playing," he joked.

Greg laughed, but I said, "Not funny."

Julie didn't seem to think it was funny, either. But she still had her hands over her ears, so maybe she hadn't heard him.

"Happens every once in a while," Uncle Dex said. "Don't worry. It doesn't have anything to do with your band. Actually, they started a couple of weeks ago and have been getting progressively louder. You guys came in at just the right time for the crescendo."

"What's a crescendo?" Greg asked.

"It's a musical term," Julie explained. "For when music or whatever sound you're talking about gets louder and louder and louder and finally hits the peak of loudness."

"So what started it?" I asked.

Uncle Dex shrugged. "Hard to say. In fact, I can't say at all. Maybe you could go ask Mrs. Strentz."

"The lady who owns Dog and Suds?" I asked.

"She's the one," Uncle Dex said. "Now if you'll excuse me . . ." He picked up a couple of earplugs from the front desk and stuck them in his ears.

"Got any more of those?" Greg asked, but Uncle Dex just smiled and shook his head.

"What are we going to do now?" Julie asked.

"I guess what Uncle Dex said," I answered. "Go ask Mrs. Strentz what's going on."

"And see if she can get those dogs to shut up," Greg said.

"Don't you think she would have done that already if she could?" Julie asked.

"Well, at least let's go outside where it might be a little quieter," I said, so we did.

As it turned out, we didn't have to go next door to talk to Mrs. Strentz because she was already out on the sidewalk, too, standing close to the curb on Caroline Street, which is one of the main streets in downtown Fredericksburg. She was glaring back at her own store and muttering to herself.

"Hi, Mrs. Strentz," I said, walking up to her. She was around my mom's age, and she looked tired, the same as my mom often does, though my mom's reason is that she has

MS. Mrs. Strentz was probably tired from wrestling dogs into their dog baths all day.

I introduced myself. "I'm Anderson Carter. Uncle Dex is my uncle."

Mrs. Strentz nodded. "Nice to meet you, Anderson. I knew your Pop Pop, too."

Pop Pop was my mom and Uncle Dex's dad. He used to own the Kitchen Sink before he died. I gestured to my friends and said, "And this is Greg and this is Julie."

Mrs. Strentz nodded at them, then she went back to glaring at the Dog and Suds. I called it glaring anyway. Julie insisted later that what Mrs. Strentz was doing was *glowering*, but I was pretty sure those were the same thing. Julie always liked to use the bigger word, though, given the opportunity, or even when there wasn't an opportunity.

"What's going on with your dogs?" I asked Mrs. Strentz, pressing on even though it was obvious she wanted to be left alone.

She sighed. "They're going crazy, that's what's going on with the dogs."

"Uncle Dex said it happens sometimes," I persisted, hoping she'd at least tell us something. "How long does it usually last?"

"It happens the same time every year. Started a couple weeks ago. And it lasts until the middle of December, so long enough to chase a lot of my customers away," Mrs. Strentz said. "Which isn't so great for business."

"What happens then?" Greg asked.

Mrs. Strentz gave a little shrug. "Then they stop barking. Or at least they go back to their normal barking, which is music to my ears."

"But you don't know what gets them started?" Julie asked.

Mrs. Strentz brushed a lock of hair off her forehead with the back of her hand. She had on her yellow dog-washing gloves. "I have a theory," she said.

"Do you mind telling us your theory?" Greg asked. He seemed genuinely curious. I just wanted her to get the dogs quiet, though it didn't look as if that was going to happen any time soon.

Mrs. Strentz pulled up her gloves like she was getting ready to march back into the Dog and Suds and fight somebody.

"A ghost," she said. "That's my theory. An annoying, frustrating, restless, hostile, belligerent, obnoxious, irritating, dog-agitating ghost."

"Oh no!" I blurted out. Another ghost already? We hadn't even taken anything out of that mysterious trunk in Uncle Dex's basement, which was how things had gotten started with the first three ghosts we'd encountered.

"Oh, yes," Mrs. Strentz said back. "Come on inside and see for yourselves."

Julie was the first one in. Greg followed her because Greg always follows her. I hung back until Mrs. Strentz motioned me to come, too. She practically had to drag me inside where the dog barking had gotten even louder, which didn't seem possible.

Then again, a lot of things lately that didn't seem possible had turned out to be not only possible, but all too real.

As I stumbled through the door to the Dog and Suds I muttered to myself, "Well, here we go again."

CHAPTER 2

The dogs continued barking like crazy for a few minutes longer, and then, as suddenly as they'd started, they stopped. The silence felt almost as loud — or I guess intense — as the noise had been just a minute before.

"That's strange," Mrs. Strentz said. "I don't remember that ever happening before."

We were in the reception area where people sat on benches with their dogs, waiting for Mrs. Strentz or one of her workers to take them into a back room or down into the basement for their baths and haircuts and nail trims and whatever else they did in there. Maybe doggie massage. The reception area had every kind of leash and collar and dog sweater and dog toy and dog treat imaginable.

Greg picked up a furry purple dog collar and tried it on. "Hey," he said. "We could all wear these when we perform. Sort of our signature."

"And change our name to the Dogs of War?" I asked.

"I think that name's already taken," Julie said, not getting that I was being sarcastic. I made a note to myself to work on that — on being more obvious when trying to say something sarcastic.

"I should keep you kids around all the time," Mrs. Strentz said. "You must be good luck. Maybe you chased the ghost away."

"How did we do that?" Greg asked, putting the collar back.

"Wish I knew," Mrs. Strentz said, and then she said it again. "I wish I knew."

•   •   •

We hung out at the Dog and Suds for a little while with Mrs. Strentz, looking around upstairs and then heading down to the basement, where there were several cages, and stainless steel tables for washing the dogs, and hoses and a drain on the floor. It felt like a dungeon, but the dogs all seemed happy enough now — and still relatively quiet. I was surprised that there were only three of them, as loud as they'd been when they were barking. One was a black Labrador, one was a dachshund, and one was a mutt beagle. Greg and Julie went right over and petted them, and even let the dogs lick their hands and faces.

I like dogs okay, but I'm not exactly thrilled about the idea of an animal slobbering on me, so I kept my distance. Also, I don't like to get dog hair all over my clothes. Julie and Greg didn't seem to mind much. Julie even kissed one.

Then she turned to Mrs. Strentz and asked, "Can you tell us more about the dog-barking issue?"

"Well, there's all the barking, of course — and it definitely gets louder over time. But something else, too," Mrs. Strentz said. "It's hard to explain, but it's just that, well, things seem to go missing and I look all over for them and they end up being right in front of me the whole time. And some mornings when I come into work, things seem to have been moved around, rearranged, or that's how it seems at first — only they haven't been. Also, it seems darker, like the lights are flickering off and on, even though they're not. It's like if you're blinking a lot, only you're not aware of it.

And the dogs go crazy, of course. You've heard that —
though I still don't understand why they stopped. I'm just
hoping that they don't start up again when you kids leave."

"Anything else?" Julie asked. "I mean, have you ever seen
or heard this ghost you say is here somewhere?"

Mrs. Strentz sighed. "Now I know you kids think I'm
just crazy, don't you? Thinking it's a ghost."

"Oh, no, Mrs. Strentz," Greg reassured her. "Not at all.
We believe in ghosts. Definitely. In fact —"

I cut him off before he said anything else that might give
away the truth about us and ghosts — or at least ghosts of
war: that we could talk to them, and had become friends
with three of them so far. "In fact, we named our band the
Ghosts of War," I said.

"Nice," Mrs. Strentz said. "Anyway, there is something
else. A couple of things, actually. I feel as though someone is
watching me. It's such a strong feeling that I keep turning to
look, only nobody's there. A few times I heard footsteps —
upstairs when I was in the basement, and in the basement
when I was upstairs. At least three people I've had working
for me over the years reported the same thing — hearing
footsteps, feeling as though they're being watched."

"Pretty spooky," Greg said.

"And noisy," Mrs. Strentz added.

"Anything else?" I asked.

"Just one thing," she said. "A voice. Only a few times, but I heard it. Or thought I heard it. Or imagined or hallucinated I heard it."

"What's it say?" Julie asked.

Mrs. Strentz hesitated, then answered. "Where's my little brother."

We waited to see if there was anything more. "Is that it?" Julie asked. "Where's my little brother?"

"Yes," Mrs. Strentz said. "Only less like a question, and more like an order."

"Like, 'Where's my little brother!'" Greg commanded.

Mrs. Strentz nodded, then led us back upstairs. She thanked us for coming in, and then gave us each a hug as she also thanked us for getting the dogs to stop barking and howling. "Even if it's just for this little while," she said.

They started right back up again the minute we left.

•   •   •

Uncle Dex still had his earplugs in, but he took them out to ask us what we'd found out from Mrs. Strentz. We had to shout to tell him — or at least we did until he led us over to some chairs near the far wall, which was the wall between the Kitchen Sink and the Dog and Suds. The minute we sat down over there, the barking subsided again, like a wave receding from the beach, only not coming back in right away.

"Interesting," Uncle Dex said, though we didn't know if he meant what Mrs. Strentz had told us or the dogs suddenly quieting down.

"What is?" Greg asked.

"Well, she says it happens around this time every year, right? Starting the middle of November?" Uncle Dex asked.

"Right," I said.

"And the middle of November — November 17, 1862, to be exact — was the date the first wave of Union forces arrived across the Rappahannock River from here, in Stafford County — preparing to attack Fredericksburg," Uncle Dex continued.

"Uh, right," I said. "We studied it in school in our unit on the Civil War, but I don't remember the exact date."

Julie interrupted me. "That is the correct date," she said. "General Burnside had just been given command of Union forces and marched his troops to Stafford County, like you said. It was supposed to be a sneak attack — they would cross the river into Fredericksburg and then march fifty miles south to Richmond, which was the Confederate capital, and there wouldn't be anybody to stop them."

"How come?" Greg asked.

"Because Robert E. Lee and the Confederate army thought the Union troops were still way west of here, near the Shenandoah Mountains," Julie said. "Only their big surprise plan didn't work out, because General Burnside and his troops couldn't cross the river. Turns out, all the bridges had been blown up weeks before — just in case the Union ever tried anything like that. So General Burnside and a hundred thousand of his men were just stuck on the Stafford County side of the Rappahannock for three weeks, waiting on the general in charge of supplies back in Washington, DC, to send down pontoons so they could build temporary bridges. That gave Lee plenty of time to find out what was going on and move his Confederate troops to Fredericksburg."

Greg wanted to know what pontoons were and Julie quickly explained. "They're these long, boat-looking things that float," she said. "The supply troops transported hundreds of them here on wagons. They weighed, like, a ton each — big enough to hold the weight of troops and horses and wagons and cannons. The idea was to lay the pontoons side-by-side all the way across the river and nail boards on top of them to build temporary bridges."

Greg and I looked at her, impressed once again by how smart she was. And *I* was supposed to be the big history buff. I actually knew all that, too, but remembering all the details, well, nobody could do that quite like Julie. Uncle Dex was impressed, as well.

"And," Uncle Dex continued again, "I'm pretty sure the barking in years past went on — well, off and on — until the middle of December, which is a long time to have to listen to that much howling, even from the place next door."

"Yeah," I said. "Mrs. Strentz told us that, too. But so what?"

"So that's when the First Battle of Fredericksburg actually took place," Julie responded. "Not until the middle of December. Starting on December 11, in fact, when the Army of the Potomac — that was the biggest branch of the Union army — was finally able to cross the river. The actual battle was on December 13."

"And ending on December 15 with Burnside ordering the Union army to retreat back across the river," Uncle Dex finished. "Which is about when the dogs next door stop making their infernal racket, or at least that's how it's been in the past. Don't know why I didn't think about this before. So could be what you have here isn't just a ghost, but a ghost from the Civil War."

I swallowed nervously. "Uh, does that mean you believe in ghosts, Uncle Dex?"

He laughed. "In a town with as much history as this one, I guess you'd be crazy not to. But who knows? Maybe those dogs just don't like the change in season and want to let everybody know it."

CHAPTER 3

Julie, who is one of the most serious people I know, had been working on being not quite so serious, and when we got back down to the basement she told us a joke.

"I bet you guys don't know why ghosts make bad liars."

Greg and I looked at each other and shrugged.

Julie got this big grin on her face. "Because you can see right through them!"

We groaned, of course. Somebody else made a noise, too.

We whirled around to see a man — or more like a teenager — in a dirty blue Union army uniform, his tattered hat cocked to one side like it had been knocked over there and never straightened.

"Where is my little brother?!" he demanded.

We were so caught off guard that nobody could speak right away, not even Julie.

The ghost was standing over the old trunk, as if looking for something. The lid was open and there was a strange golden light inside. He took a step toward us — a menacing step, or that's how it seemed — and said it, or demanded it, again.

"Where is my little brother?!"

We were all still scared speechless, trying to think of something, anything, to say back.

The ghost stood firm and waited, hands on the hips of his dirty pants, which seemed a couple of sizes too big. The uniform coat seemed too big, too. For some reason there was a sprig of wilted green leaves tucked into the collar. The ghost was short and it was obvious that he didn't shave or didn't need to — that's how young he was. But he still looked like he wanted to fight somebody. I wanted to assure him that we weren't part of the Confederate army. I mean, I was from the South, sure, but I wasn't a Rebel or anything. I didn't even like the Rebels, or what they stood for and what they fought for.

But it didn't seem like the time or place to tell the Union soldier — or ghost — all that.

Julie finally found her voice. "We don't know where your little brother is," she said calmly — way calmer than Greg or I could have been, or were likely to be for another hour. "And we don't know who he is. But maybe we can help you figure it out."

"Help me?" the ghost said, his voice so high that I thought he could almost pass for a girl.

"Yes, help you," Julie said. "We've helped some other ghosts. They had things in that trunk." She pointed and the ghost turned to look at the trunk, which was still open, and still giving off that golden light.

Julie continued, "Is there something of yours in there?"

The ghost continued staring for a minute, and then nodded. "I lost it in the battle, but there it is." He thought for a minute, then added, "I can't pick it up."

"Can you tell us what it is?" Julie asked.

"They told us to fix bayonets," the ghost said. "That's all I remember."

I knew all about bayonets, which are like long knives, or more like the end of a spear, and you attach it to the end of your gun so you can use it as a weapon for close fighting. "Fix bayonets" is the order they give when soldiers are supposed to get out their bayonets and put them on their rifles.

"Is there a bayonet in the trunk?" Julie asked. "Is that what you're missing?"

"It wouldn't have mattered if I'd had it," the ghost said, not answering Julie's question. "Nobody got close enough. Nobody at all."

And with that the ghost vanished, the golden light blinked out, the trunk lid slammed shut on its own, and the dogs next door started up their barking once again.

Needless to say, we didn't get any more practicing done that day, but we did all dive into the trunk to search for the ghost's bayonet. We didn't have to look long, though, because there it was, sitting right on top, as if it had been placed there in anticipation of our searching for it.

Julie picked it up. It was rusted steel, a long, thin blade at one end and a sort of cylinder or socket on the other to slide over the end of the barrel on a soldier's musket in the Civil War.

"So that's what she was looking for," Julie said.

"You mean *he*," Greg corrected her.

"Yes. That's what I said," Julie replied.

Greg and I both shook our heads.

Julie gave an awkward laugh. "I guess I did. I don't know why. That's weird."

"Forget it," Greg said. "We're all shook up and tired, and if I have to listen to those dogs bark for one more minute, I think my head's going to fall off."

"Yeah, maybe we should call it a day," I said, already picking up my book bag and heading for the door. We usually left our instruments in the practice room, though Julie was always getting on me and Greg about taking our guitars home and practicing more there. Today she didn't say anything, though. She still seemed kind of confused.

"Hey, do you think we should give the bayonet to your uncle?" Greg asked. "You remember how upset he was about the hand grenade."

I thought about it and decided we could probably just hang on to the bayonet, though. I mean, a rusty bayonet wasn't going to explode or anything, and it looked cool.

Uncle Dex was already closing up shop when we got upstairs. The dogs were still barking. "I'll be setting up a music system tomorrow," he told us. "Speakers all over the store. I'm hoping I can drown out at least some of the barking and howling, and actually have a few customers not only come in but stay a while and buy something, too."

"We'll see you tomorrow afternoon, Uncle Dex," I said.

"And I'll bring some music you can play over your new system," Julie said.

"Just as long as it's good old-time rock and roll," Uncle Dex said. "Has to be loud enough to do the trick, so no soft classical."

"Plus, you just like old-time rock and roll," I added. Uncle Dex just winked.

Julie, still in a daze or something, climbed on her bike and rode home without saying anything else to Greg or me. Greg and I rode most of the way home together since we lived close to each other.

"Was Julie acting a little strange?" Greg asked, puffs of his breath appearing in the chilly air. "Didn't you think?"

"Julie's always a little strange," I said. "What I thought was strange was, um, let me see — oh yeah, we met another ghost and this one's from the Civil War!"

I was working on being sarcastic again, and this time it seemed to come through.

"Well, you don't have to be that way about it," Greg said.

"You have to admit it's still really weird for ghosts to just show up like that," I said.

"Yeah," Greg said. "But this one sure is different from the others. I mean, always before we found the thing — the navy pea coat, the dud hand grenade, the medic's kit — and *then* the ghost showed up."

"I suppose it's like Julie keeps telling us," I said. "These ghosts are all different — they're people, too — and this one seems to be living right next door. At least in November and December."

"These mysteries — they're exhausting," Greg said. "But I guess call me tonight if the new one shows up in your bedroom like all the other ones did."

I shuddered, thinking about the Civil War ghost doing just that. I wasn't afraid, exactly. I just didn't have a warm, fuzzy feeling about this new ghost. Not at all.

· · ·

Mom and Dad were waiting for me in the living room when I got home. "Don't take your shoes off, Anderson," Dad said. "We need to take your mom to the hospital."

My heart sank. I went straight over to Mom on the couch and hugged her. "Don't worry, sweetie," she said. "I don't think it's anything serious."

Mom has MS — multiple sclerosis — which is what they call an autoimmune disease where her body kind of breaks down and leaves her really weak sometimes, and sometimes some of her organs don't work right, and sometimes she can get really stiff in her muscles, like she's almost paralyzed. There are drugs they can give her, and different therapies, and it's better sometimes and worse other times. They can't cure it, though.

"What happened?" I asked.

"Oh, well, my leg just seemed to give out from under me a little while ago," Mom said. "I was in the kitchen, actually feeling good for a change, but then the next thing I know I fell. Your father came home and found me on the floor. I don't know if I hit my head."

"Which is why we're going to the hospital," Dad interrupted. "To get it checked out. So let's get going, you two."

I had this sick feeling in my stomach for the next few hours as we sat in the emergency room, and then waited a long time in an examination room for a doctor to come in to see Mom, and then while we waited for an X-ray on her leg, which didn't show anything, and an MRI to make sure there wasn't anything to worry about from maybe hitting her head.

Everything came back negative, except that Mom seemed to get weaker and weaker while we were there and they decided to keep her at the hospital overnight for observation. It was midnight by then, and Dad and I didn't even bother to go home. We just slept in chairs in Mom's room. We never even ate dinner, but after everything that had gone on that day — worrying about Mom, and the whole business with the dogs and the Civil War ghost before that — I don't think I could have eaten anything anyway.

CHAPTER 4

I skipped school the next day to stay at the hospital with Mom. She told me this wasn't necessary, but I was still worried and didn't want to be away from her.

"You don't need to keep checking on me, Anderson," Mom said when I asked her for about the millionth time how she was feeling. "I'm fine. The nurses are right out there in the nurses' station if anything happens. And nothing's going to happen."

"But you fell," I said.

"And I'm sure I'll fall again some time," Mom said. "I just need to be more careful. That's all. This isn't going to go away. We just need to keep doing what we're doing."

"Which is what?" I asked.

"Which is continuing to adapt," Mom said. "Keep learning how to live with MS. Not be afraid to live our lives. And I certainly don't want you to be so afraid for me that you don't live *your* life."

"I do," I said. "I mean, I think I do."

Mom smiled. "I just mean I want you to keep doing the things that you're supposed to do, like going to school and helping around the house, and also the things you like to do, like your band and hanging out with your friends, and solving those history mysteries with Greg and Julie."

"Those are for school," I said quickly. "I mean, mostly."

Mom nodded. "Now scoot. I'm tired and since they're just observing me I want you to go do something."

"Like what?" I asked. Mom dug in her pocketbook and handed me some money. "Go down to the cafeteria and get something to eat. Or buy yourself a treat. Go wander around. Do some exploring."

"Are you sure you'll be okay by yourself?" I asked. "I don't mind staying. I can just keep sitting right here in the sleep chair."

I was sitting on the edge of Mom's hospital bed while we

talked. She reached over and pushed me off, which caught me totally by surprise. I landed on my butt on the floor.

"Are you hurt?" she asked, trying not to laugh. I shook my head, though my tailbone was a little sore.

"Then go," she ordered. So I took the money and left.

I actually was really hungry, so I ordered a big breakfast in the hospital cafeteria plus two cartons of chocolate milk. After I ate I went outside to text Greg and Julie about what had happened to my mom. I had a couple of texts and voice mails from both of them: Greg wondering where I was and why I wasn't responding to his earlier messages, Julie telling me stuff she was reading about the Civil War and the Battle of Fredericksburg.

"While the Union army was stuck on the wrong side of the river for those three weeks waiting for pontoons, Robert E. Lee and his Army of Northern Virginia had plenty of time to move in and set up their defenses on the hills just south of Fredericksburg," she explained in one voice mail.

As I was standing there, reading and listening to the messages from Julie and Greg, I realized the hospital was built on one of the hills where the Confederate forces had probably dug in, with all the advantages of holding the higher ground. I remembered from school that the Rebels' defensive line ran for several miles along the ridge of these hills, starting around where I was standing and running east. Plus, there was a national park in town where the most important parts of the battle were fought. I could see the river just to the north, half a mile away, and I could even see one of the bridges — the Falmouth Bridge — that the Confederates destroyed. It dawned on me as I surveyed the area why everything that happened in the Battle of Fredericksburg, everything the Union army did — or didn't do when they had the chance — was such a disaster in the making.

·　·　·

Eventually, I went back to Mom's room for a couple of hours and hung around while they did some more tests and while she napped some, but she finally kicked me out again and told me to go meet my friends and do something. Band practice. Whatever. She insisted that she was fine.

"Your dad will be back this evening," she said. "We'll all meet up back here for a delicious hospital dinner."

It was cold out, nearly three in the afternoon. School would be out soon. I walked home and got my bike, then rode over to the Kitchen Sink after texting Julie and Greg that I'd be there.

Uncle Dex looked up when I walked in. The dogs next door were barking, though it didn't seem to be quite as loud as the day before. "Hey, Anderson!" Uncle Dex said, or shouted, even though he probably didn't need to. "How's everything? I talked to your mom. She sounds a lot better. Glad everything's going to be okay."

"Thanks," I said. Uncle Dex is Mom's brother. They're really close, and since Uncle Dex isn't married he comes over to our house a lot for dinner and stuff. He had come by the hospital and hung out with us for a while the night before.

"Oh, somebody came by looking for you," he said. "I almost forgot."

"Was it Greg?" I asked, though if it had been Uncle Dex probably would have already said. Plus, I doubted Greg could have gotten there so fast from school.

"No," he answered. "And not Julie, either."

"Well, who then?" I asked. For a second I was worried that it might have been the Civil War ghost, but of course Uncle Dex wouldn't or couldn't have known about him.

"Not sure," he said. "A younger kid. I'm guessing a grade below you guys."

"A fifth grader?" I couldn't imagine who it could have been.

"Maybe," said Uncle Dex. He looked toward the front of the store as the door opened. "But you can probably just ask her yourself, because there she is."

I turned to look, too, and nearly fell over when I saw: It was Belman's little sister — the one we met the night of Julie's piano recital that I wrote about in one of my notebooks, "AWOL in North Africa." She was just standing there grinning at me, and she might have been a little fifth grader and all, but it was about the scariest-looking grin I'd ever seen.

"Hello, Anderson," she said in a fake-sweet voice.

"Hello, uh, Little Belman," I said.

Before I could think of anything else to say, or a way to get her to go away, Uncle Dex interrupted. "Why don't you kids head on down to the basement? I've got work to do up here."

And the next thing I knew, without me even inviting her, the scary little Belman was following me downstairs to our practice room. I couldn't for the life of me guess why she was there, or what she wanted, and I wasn't too sure I wanted to find out.

CHAPTER 5

"My name is not Little Belman," Little Belman said as soon as we got there. "It's Deedee. And don't forget it."

I just looked at her. She was small for a fifth grader, with long blond hair pulled back in a ponytail. But she still looked tough.

"Okay, Deedee," I said. "I'll try to remember."

"You better," she snapped. "And I'll tell you why I'm here. It's because I know it was you, or your friend, who attacked my brother at the piano recital."

"You mean the eggs that fell on his head?" I asked. "And the rubber chicken?"

She just glared at me, because of course that's what she was talking about. Greg had secretly dropped all that on Belman while he was onstage performing, but nobody had actually seen him do it. It was to get back at Belman for shooting Greg with a rubber chicken out of a potato cannon. And for shooting Greg and me with potatoes.

"My brother is a nice guy," Deedee continued. "Too nice to do anything about it. But I'm not as nice as him."

I nearly fell over again when she said that, because Belman was about the not-nicest person I'd ever met. But no matter what, I wasn't about to admit to anything concerning Greg and the rubber chicken to Belman's little sister, especially since she was claiming to be even worse than him.

"I'm sorry your brother got clobbered," I said, not sure what else to say. Maybe a joke would help. "But I guess now we know which one came first."

"What are you talking about?" Deedee asked, exasperated. "Which *what* came first?"

"You know, the whole chicken or the egg thing," I said. "The egg hit your brother first and then the chicken. Not that I know who did it. But so now we know the answer to that age-old question: Which came first, the chicken or the egg?"

"I think you're a moron," Deedee said.

Somebody stepped up behind her when she said that. Somebody in a tattered blue uniform from the Civil War. The ghost!

"It ain't polite to talk so ugly to people as that," the ghost said to Deedee.

Deedee whirled around, saw the ghost, and screamed. Then she bolted out of the room and up the stairs, still screaming. I heard her thunder through the store, making all kinds of noise.

"Oh great!" I said to the ghost. "Why'd you have to scare her like that?"

"She wasn't one of yours?" the ghost asked. "I thought she was in your band."

"No," I said. "She's not. And now what are we going to do? She'll tell everybody!"

The ghost didn't have time to answer because Uncle Dex came rushing downstairs. "Anderson!" he shouted as he came through the door. "What in the world happened down here?"

The ghost had already vanished and I didn't know what to say, so I just blurted out the obvious. "She thought she saw a ghost and got scared and ran out of here."

"I heard all that," Uncle Dex said. "As loud as she was yelling, I'd be surprised if every shop owner and shopper downtown didn't hear her. So what made her think there was a ghost down here?"

We both looked around. The dogs next door started barking again and I realized they'd stopped once again when the ghost showed up — but they were only quiet for as long as he was here. "Well, it is kind of spooky," I said. "You know, cobwebs and shadows. And it's, like, a really old building. Maybe she just *thought* she saw a ghost. I don't know. One minute we were talking, and the next minute she ran out of here screaming."

"Are you sure you didn't do or say anything to scare her?" Uncle Dex asked. "On purpose?"

"No," I said. "I swear."

Uncle Dex shook his head. "You kids." That was all. Or just about all. "The next time you see her, you apologize for scaring her," he said. "Even if you didn't mean to. You must have said something that got her all worked up like that."

Julie and Greg came in just then. "What's going on?" Greg asked.

"We just saw Belman's little sister running down the sidewalk," Julie added. "And boy, can she move fast."

"She thought she saw a ghost," Uncle Dex said, then headed back upstairs.

I filled them in after he left. Greg groaned. "Oh no! What are we going to do now? She'll tell everybody."

"But nobody will believe her," Julie said, already sizing up the situation. "They'll just think she got frightened being in an old scary building, and that she got hysterical, and that's all. And if anybody asks us, that's what we'll say, too. She's just a little kid after all."

"She's only one grade below us," I pointed out.

"Yeah, but she's still in elementary school and we're in middle school, and that makes all the difference," Julie said.

"Well, I just hope she didn't scare the real ghost away," Greg said. "Because I've been doing a *lot* of research and I'd hate for it to go to waste."

"So what do we do now?" I asked. "Even if nobody believes Little Belman about seeing the ghost, they're going to be asking a lot of questions."

"We have to get out in front of this," Julie said.

"What does that mean?" Greg asked.

"It means we address it before somebody can ask us about it," Julie responded. "We tell our story first, and that becomes the story."

"And just what exactly is our story?" I asked.

Julie thought hard for a minute, and then smiled. "We

call Little Belman's parents and apologize. We tell them that it was Greg, dressed up like a Civil War ghost, and he'd been hiding and then he jumped out and scared her. We tell them it was just supposed to be a dumb prank, and we didn't know she would get so freaked-out."

"Brilliant!" Greg announced before I could say anything. Julie turned her smile to him now, and I was pretty sure Greg blushed, which was definitely weird.

But then Greg added, "Uh, couldn't we say it was Anderson, though? I don't want to get in trouble or anything."

I shook my head. "Can't be me. I was the one talking to Little Belman — or getting threatened by Little Belman — when the ghost showed up."

Greg looked back at Julie. She knew what he was going to ask before he even said it. "Can't be me, either," she said. "I'm a girl."

"Oh yeah," Greg said, blushing again. "I mean, I knew that."

The ghost chose that moment to show back up again, suddenly standing right next to Julie and Greg and me, as if it had been the four of us talking casually together all along. And once again, as if on cue, the dogs next door hushed.

"I didn't like that girl," the ghost said. "And if you ask me, little as she is she still might be a Rebel spy."

CHAPTER 6

We all stood there and looked at him for a second. He couldn't have been much older than us, but I'd read that during the Civil War they took soldiers who were in their teens, and some lied about their age and were actually even younger.

"Uh, I guess we should introduce ourselves," I said, and I started to say our names but the ghost cut me off.

"You're Anderson. That boy's name is Greg. And the girl is Julie. I already knew all that. Nice to meet you."

"Nice to meet you, too," Greg said. "But we don't know your name yet."

The ghost winced. "Well, dang it, I don't know it either, so we're even. But that ain't why I'm here."

"You're looking for your little brother, right?" Greg asked. He took off his beanie and his red hair sort of sprouted up around his head from static electricity.

"First time I seen you with that thing off," the ghost said. "Didn't know you were a redhead. And yeah, I been looking for my brother and I need you all to help me find him, and that's the long and the short of it."

"Do you know his name?" I asked. "That would be a big help."

"'Course I do," the ghost practically barked. "He's my brother, ain't he? My own flesh and blood." He seemed to be getting all worked up, but then he stopped. "Dang. It's right there on the tip of my tongue. My little brother. We're in the same unit, doggone it. But I all of a sudden can't seem to remember . . ."

He trailed off.

"That's okay," I said quickly. "We know how it is when you're a ghost. How hard it is to remember stuff, like even your own name. But we can help you. We have a lot of experience in this sort of thing."

The ghost looked doubtful. "You're just kids," he said.

"No offense," Greg said, "but you don't look like you're a lot older than us."

The ghost drew himself up, standing as tall as he could, but he was just a couple of inches taller than Julie, who was the tallest of the three of us. "Bigger than any of you," the ghost said. "And I been in the war. I bet you never been in the war."

"We didn't mean any disrespect," said Julie. "But we would like to try to help you if we can."

That seemed to calm the ghost down. "I thank you for the offer. Does kind of feel like I been waiting for somebody like you all for a while. A long, long while."

"It's been more than a hundred and fifty years since the war ended," I said. "We call it the Civil War."

"That long?" the ghost said. "Who won? I pray it was the Union, but after what happened here at Fredericksburg, over at Marye's Heights, well, I just don't know how we could prevail."

"But you did!" Greg blurted. "I mean *we* did! America did. I mean the Union."

"Well, glory, glory, hallelujah!" the ghost exclaimed. His grin was practically wider than his face. "Thank you for telling me. Would of hated to hear there was still a Confederate States of America, but it sure was in doubt when I was fighting."

"Do you remember anything about that?" Julie asked. "Anything about the Battle of Fredericksburg?"

"'Course I do," the ghost said. "You think I've just been lying around all this time forgetting things? Why I remember every single detail just like it was yesterday."

"Like what?" I asked, eager to hear. Greg and Julie leaned in, too. The ghost might not remember his own name, or his brother's, but it sure sounded like he remembered something.

But the ghost shook his head. "Dang it. There it is again, right on the tip of my tongue, but just won't come out." He stomped his foot like a little kid and ground his teeth together. I thought he might throw a tantrum. But then he sagged, like he was losing air. "Well, I guess some days I don't remember," he said sadly. "Like today."

"Do you at least remember the unit you were in?" Julie asked. "That would be a great start. We could do some research to see what brothers were in that unit. I bet they have that sort of thing recorded."

The ghost blinked. And blinked again. And kept blinking, as if it would somehow trigger a memory — any memory at this point. That wide grin had totally disappeared, and now he just looked young and sad.

"What day is it?" he asked, finally saying *something*. "I mean the date. What date is it? What month and what number day of the month?"

"December 5," I said.

He nodded. "Now we're getting somewhere. That was the day it started snowing. The year of 1862. Came from out of nowhere. We'd been stuck across the river from Fredericksburg for a couple of weeks, just waiting. We weren't prepared for snow, not at all, though we should have been. Only it had been so warm the whole time we were here.

"And I'll tell you what else I remember about December 5, 1862 — that I was on scout duty, near the river's edge. The Rappahannock River. The Rebels had blown up the bridges, including this one at a little town just a little ways to the north. The locals called it Foul Mouth. You know it?"

"Oh, sure," Greg said. "Only it's not Foul Mouth, it's Falmouth. Which I guess sounds kind of the same."

"That's on the north side of the river, just maybe a mile and a half from here," I added. "The Confederates dynamited the Falmouth Bridge, so the Union troops — you guys — couldn't cross. They also blew up the Chatham

Bridge, which is just a couple of blocks from here, and the railroad bridge, which is just a half a mile east of where we are. But I guess you knew all that."

"Where's the river from here?" the ghost asked.

I pointed north. "Just one block over," I said.

"And where are we exactly?"

"We're in Fredericksburg. Downtown, on Caroline Street. At my uncle's junk shop — I mean antique store," I said. "It's called the Kitchen Sink."

"And next door is the dog shop," the ghost said, not asking.

Greg answered anyway. "The Dog and Suds," he said. "That's what it's called. They groom pets over there."

"Maybe so," the ghost said. "But it's where I live, too." He looked at himself — at his dusty blue uniform, tattered and faded and a couple of sizes too big. "If you can call this living."

None of us knew what to say in response, so I changed the subject back to what he remembered.

"You said you were on a scout mission, or scout duty, or whatever," I said. "Across the river, in Stafford. Near Falmouth?"

"That's right," the ghost said. "And could see the Johnny Rebs, too, on the other side of the river, out scouting for us,

I guess. Of course they knew where we were the same as we knew where they were. So finally we came out from the trees and hollered over to them. And they hollered back."

"What did you say?" Greg asked.

The ghost laughed. "Probably told them they ought to just go on ahead and surrender, 'cause as soon as we crossed that river it was going to be all over for them and the rest of Robert E. Lee's army."

"And what did they say back?" I asked.

"Best I can recall they asked if we had any sugar. Or anything else we wanted to trade."

"Trade for what?" Greg asked. I was just surprised that the Confederates would even have something like that on their minds, when the two armies were on opposite sides of the Rappahannock River, getting ready for what turned out to be one of the bloodiest battles of the Civil War. But I guess they were just hungry.

"Tobacco," the ghost said. "Once the war broke out, there wasn't much tobacco for folks up north, and lot of guys in the Union army were dippers and smokers and spitters."

"That's disgusting," Julie said. "I hope you didn't do any of that, as young as you are. Or were."

"Maybe I did and maybe I didn't," the ghost said, suddenly sounding defensive. "Anyway, I'm grown up and I can make my own decisions and ain't none of anybody else's business."

"Sorry," Julie said quickly. "But, well, it's not good for you, you know."

"It isn't?" the ghost said. "First time I've heard of that. Who says it ain't good for you?"

"The surgeon general," I said. "It's written all over packs of cigarettes. And it's on TV about how bad it is for you. Not just cigarettes, but the other stuff that you mentioned, too. For dipping and spitting and stuff."

The ghost was perplexed. "Surgeon general? Never heard of any general by that name. And everybody knows TB is bad for you. Heck, TB can kill a person, and I guess I should know."

"No, not *TB*," Julie corrected him. "I said *TV. Television*. It's like radio, only there are pictures."

"What's radio?" the ghost asked.

Greg answered. "Just this thing that can carry people's voices and music and stuff so you can hear it when you're driving in your car. Unless you're on your cell phone, or have your music player out and your earbuds in, and . . ."

"Could you start speaking in English?" the ghost interrupted. "'Cause I don't have any idea what you're talking about right now."

"Modern stuff," Julie explained. "We'll just let it go at that. But you mentioned TB. That's tuberculosis, right? Contagious disease that destroys your lungs?"

"That's what they call it," the ghost said. "Or else consumption. Or else the White Plague."

"And you said you should know it can kill a person?" Julie continued.

The ghost got quiet again. His voice was practically a whisper. "Right. I did say that." He was fading — not just his voice, but all of him. I hoped we had time for one more question.

"But why did you say it?" I asked.

"'Cause," he said, now mostly gone, just sort of the outline of him left for us to see, and not even quite that. "How do you think Frank and me got to be orphans? It happened to Mama and Papa. They got sent to the sanatorium but they never came home again."

And then he wasn't even an outline — just gone. Greg still shouted after him, though: "Is Frank your brother? Did you just remember? And what's your last name?"

· 46 ·

I couldn't help myself. I shouted after him, too, even though I knew it wouldn't do any good. "And what was your unit in the war?"

The only answer we got was the dogs next door, barking their heads off yet again.

CHAPTER 7

I had to get back to check on Mom at the hospital, but Julie insisted — again — that we had to get ahead of the thing with Little Belman first. We looked up Belman's address and fortunately it wasn't too far, past the train station and down near the city dock — just half a mile from Uncle Dex's store. Downtown turned more residential down that way, with a lot of really old houses built before the Civil War.

We rode our bikes there, though the sun was already sinking low in the western sky and it was getting kind of dark. We parked our bikes in front of a newly renovated Victorian house, with a steep set of steps going up from the sidewalk. Hanging in one of the windows was a banner with a blue star in the middle.

"What's that all about?" Greg asked, meaning the blue star.

"It's what you put on your house or in your window or wherever to let people know that a member of your family is overseas in the war," I said. "I think they started it in World War I, and some people still do it today."

"Must be for Iraq and Afghanistan," Greg said. "I wonder if Belman's dad is over there."

"Maybe," I said. "Or maybe his mom."

"It couldn't be her," Julie said. "Remember, she was with them at the piano recital where Greg — I mean, where somebody — dropped the eggs and the rubber chicken on Belman's head?"

Greg laughed. I changed the subject.

"So, um, who's doing the talking when Mrs. Belman answers the door?" I asked.

Greg and I both looked at Julie. She rolled her eyes. "You guys are such babies sometimes," she said.

"Well, yeah," Greg said, not arguing with her. "But since you came up with the story — and it's a great story, don't get me wrong — and since I'm the one who supposedly did this terrible thing to this poor little kid — it just makes sense that somebody else should be the one to talk to Belman's mom."

I didn't say anything. I just wanted to get the whole thing over with so I could get to the hospital. I was feeling guilty that I'd been gone for so long from Mom. For about the hundredth time I checked my phone for text messages, but the only one was what Dad had sent me a couple of hours before saying he would meet me at Mom's room when he got off work. Of course there was no telling when that might be since Dad works in Washington, DC, and the traffic is always terrible on the interstate driving back down to Fredericksburg in the afternoon.

"Just come on," Julie said. "I'll do it."

A woman my mom's age came to the door when we knocked. She had on an oversize shirt that might have been Belman's dad's. She looked tired and sad, and like probably her short hair hadn't been brushed in a while. But maybe we'd woken her up from a nap or something.

"Can I help you?" she asked in a soft voice.

"Yes," Julie said. "I'm Julie, and this is Greg and this is Anderson."

We both said hi. Mrs. Belman nodded to us.

"We came to apologize for scaring your daughter," Julie continued, getting right to the point.

"Deedee," Mrs. Belman said, I guess just to confirm that it was the right daughter.

"Yes, that's right," Julie said. "Deedee. Anyway, she probably told you she came to our band practice downtown a little while ago and got scared because she thought she saw a ghost, but that was just Greg sort of dressed up like a ghost. It was in Anderson's uncle's store, in the basement, which is kind of spooky. Anyway, she ran away before we could tell her it was just a prank. So we're really sorry."

Mrs. Belman didn't say anything. She just blinked at us, like the ghost had done earlier. At least that's what she reminded me of. She might have been waiting for Julie to say something else, but Julie was finished.

After a few seconds, which felt like forever, Mrs. Belman frowned. "That wasn't very nice of you, to frighten someone like that. Deedee is pretty upset."

"Would you like us to apologize to her?" Greg asked. "We really are sorry."

Mrs. Belman thought about it, but then shook her head. "I'll tell her you came by to apologize. She gets very emotional sometimes, and she does tend to overreact about things." She paused. "Just promise me you won't do anything like that again. And it wouldn't hurt for you kids to be nice to Deedee. She's had a hard time making friends this year."

I wondered if that might have been part of the reason Little Belman had come by the Kitchen Sink earlier — not just to threaten us about her brother, but because secretly she was lonely and wanted to make some friends, as weird as that sounded.

We assured Mrs. Belman that we would be nice to Little Belman from now on, and we told her again how sorry we were, and we probably would have continued standing there apologizing, but she finally interrupted to thank us, and then shooed us away.

"Whew!" Julie said. "I'm glad that's over."

"Yeah," said Greg. "And I'm just glad she wasn't mad at us."

"And we didn't have to see Belman," I added. "Or Little Belman."

We turned and headed down the steep steps to our bikes. It was getting even darker and cooler now that the sun was almost all the way down. But it wasn't too cold for this time of the year, so that was a relief since I still had to ride over to the hospital.

But we weren't going to get away quite so easily, as it turned out, because a water balloon exploded on the sidewalk beside us, and then another, both splashing all over us and our bikes.

Little Belman was leaning out of a second-story window, holding yet another. "You guys are big fat liars!" she shouted. "I heard what you said to my mom! And the ghost I saw wasn't a boy, it was a girl!"

Then she threw the third water balloon, and this time her aim was better. Greg ducked but it hit him anyway, right in the back. We didn't wait to see if she had any more. We hopped on our bikes and tore away from there as fast as we could. A block away we nearly ran into Belman himself, and his three friends who we called the Three Stooges. They scattered off the sidewalk as we zoomed past. I was surprised they didn't push us off our bikes.

•　　•　　•

We didn't have time to do what Julie calls a postmortem on the attack by Little Belman, and everything else that had happened that afternoon, which was almost too much to even hold in my brain. According to Julie, a postmortem is when you go back over things to figure out how they happened and what they could mean.

I had to split off from Julie and Greg to go the hospital, and they were both late getting home, too, so we just said we'd talk to one another later, and off we went. Mom was asleep when I got to her room, but just dozing. I was going to sit down and read a book so when she woke up I could pretend I'd been there for a long time, but she opened her eyes as soon as I walked in.

"Must have been quite a band practice you guys had," she said. She smiled. I breathed a sigh of relief because she didn't seem mad or anything that I was a little late.

"Sorry we took so long," I said. "How are you feeling?"

"Well enough to go home," she said. "But they want to keep me here for one more night for observation. They didn't say anything about me having to stay in the room, though, so what do you say we take one of those hospital wheelchairs out for a spin?"

"Who's riding — me or you?" I asked, trying to be upbeat even though I was bummed she had to stay another night. "Or were you thinking we could both be in one and have a race?"

Mom laughed, which made me happy. "You push," she said. "I ride."

"What about Dad?" I asked. "He come by yet?"

"Not yet," Mom said. "And he better bring us something good to make up for it when he gets here."

"Or else what?" I asked.

Mom laughed again. "Or else if we see him while we're out joyriding in the wheelchair, we run over his foot."

Dad showed up fifteen minutes later. Lucky for him he brought donuts.

CHAPTER 8

"I've written out a list of questions," Julie said the next afternoon when we met up for band practice. My mom was out of the hospital and resting back home. She practically threw me out of the house when I got home from school because I kept checking on her and asking if she needed anything.

"Okay," Greg said. "Let's hear what you've got."

"Number one, let's start with the ghost. How could he remember that specific day — December 5, 1862 — and could also remember that his parents died from tuberculosis, but not remember his name, or what unit he was with, or where he was from?"

"That sounds like about six questions," I pointed out, but Julie ignored me and answered her own question.

"The only explanation is that, well, he's a ghost, and it's hard to remember everything right away," she said. "We've seen it before with our other ghosts. Also, he disappeared right when things seemed to be coming back to him, about his parents, and about him and his little brother being orphans, so maybe getting emotional about all that was too much for him and that's why he disappeared just then."

"Wow," Greg said. "You've already thought a lot about this."

Julie nodded. "I must have stayed up most of the night. Anyway, we're just going to have to wait for the ghost to come back to see what else he can remember."

"Wait," Greg said. "Since yesterday was the *real* December 5 — you know, in our time — and when he found that out that's when he remembered *his* December 5, maybe since today is the real December 6 now he'll be able to remember his December 6. From 1862."

"That makes sense," I said. "Plus, I bet he'll keep remembering more stuff from before December 6, too." I shook my head. "Boy, this ghost stuff can sure get complicated. They're all just so different from one another."

"Except one thing," Greg said. "Which is that it's us they keep coming back to, and we're the only ones who can see them."

"Not quite," Julie interrupted. "What about Little Belman? She saw the ghost yesterday afternoon when she came down here to confront Anderson."

"Is that on your question list?" I asked.

"Yes," she said. "And right after it is the question about why she said the ghost was a girl, not a boy."

"Yeah, that was really weird," Greg said. "Maybe she just got confused. It was probably her first ghost and she did get pretty freaked out."

"Any more questions?" I asked. "Because I don't think we have very good answers to the Little Belman questions. And I'm not too sure we've got things quite figured out about what the ghost was able to remember yesterday, either."

"I have one," Greg said. "How in the world did that little kid manage to eavesdrop on us talking to her mom, then race upstairs, fill three water balloons, and get to the window to throw them at us that fast?"

Julie shrugged. "Either she already had the water balloons waiting, or else she's just super efficient."

"Maybe she's the Flash," Greg said. "World's Fastest Man. Or Girl Flash, I guess."

"Oh, please," Julie said. "There's no such thing as the Flash. That's a comic book."

"Oh, sure," Greg said, laughing. "So we're okay believing in ghosts, but not the Flash."

"Yes, that's right," Julie said. "Ghosts are real."

"Back to Little Belman," I said. "I'm still stuck on the question about how she could see the ghost. Remember, we've seen ghosts while we were riding with Uncle Dex in his car, and we've seen them at school — or at least I have — but nobody else, not even Uncle Dex, has seen them. So why Little Belman?"

Greg pulled off his beanie and scratched his wild red hair. "I guess some people just can, and she's one of them, like us. Only she got so scared that maybe she won't see any more."

"We got scared, too," I pointed out. "At first."

"Yeah, but we got over it," Greg said. "She went home and hid in her house and filled up water balloons."

"Which, now that I think about it, she probably did to throw at the ghost if it followed her home," Julie said. "That must be why she was able to get to them so quickly and throw them at us." She looked at Greg. "And on us, in Greg's case."

"Maybe we should get back to the important business here," I said, "which is still the Battle of Fredericksburg and what happened to our ghost."

"And what happened to his little brother," Greg added.

"Right," Julie said. "So here's what I think. The ghost and his little brother were both in the Union army, and probably in the same unit, and the little brother deserted, or got killed or went missing or got captured in the battle. So that's why the ghost is still looking for him, or trying to find out what happened to him."

"The ghost must have gotten killed, too," I said. "Because, well, he's a ghost."

"Of course, Anderson," Julie responded. "That goes without saying. And like the other ghosts we've met, he must have been missing, too. And that's part of the mystery we have to solve."

"So it's a double mystery," Greg said. "The ghost *and* the ghost's little brother. Wow. We haven't had to tackle anything like this before."

"There's something else making this one difficult," Julie said. "With the other ghosts we were able to track down people who were still alive and could help us solve the mystery of what happened to them."

"But this ghost died more than a hundred and fifty years ago!" I exclaimed.

"Yep," said Greg. "Nobody still alive from back then, that's for sure."

There was a sort of shimmering in the air next to Greg, and then, like a blurry picture slowly coming into focus, the ghost finally, fully, appeared.

"Well, I'm here now, ain't I?" he said.

"Welcome back," I said, but he dismissed it with a wave of his hand.

"No time for niceness," he said. "Let's get back to the remembering. Now what day is it?"

CHAPTER 9

"It was still snowing on December 6, I remember that much," the ghost said after we told him what date it was for the actual day we were in. That seemed to be all the prompting he needed.

"They sent us back out on a scouting patrol, only this time we didn't just go down to where the bridge used to be. This time we made our way on the bank upriver a ways, to where it was lots of big rocks and rapids. You had to watch where you were walking on account of how our feet were so cold we couldn't hardly feel them, and you could step in water and not even know it. I heard about some of our boys who got frostbite and even lost some toes. Surgeons had to pull them right off."

I shuddered at the thought of that.

"I guess you guys were still waiting for the pontoons," Greg said.

The ghost made a fist and shook it at Greg. "Don't even talk to me about those pontoons! I'm still mad about the sorry bums back in Washington that fell down on the job! Word was that we could have waltzed right across that river with no Rebels on the other side to give us any trouble at all if we'd just had those pontoons earlier, when we needed them. And then we could have marched right up on Richmond and the Rebels wouldn't have had their capital anymore or their president, Mr. Jefferson Davis, and the war might have been over right then and there. If we'd only been able to cross that river in time."

"Wasn't there someplace else you could have forded the river?" I asked. "Somewhere upstream, where you could have maybe walked over on the rocks?"

"Well, sure," the ghost said. "You don't think we scouted all up and down that Rappahannock? Plenty of places troops could have gotten across, but not the cannon and not the horses and not the wagons or anything else on wheels. And you're talking about a hundred thousand of us boys in blue. It wasn't just about getting across yourself. It was about getting a whole army across. And you need bridges for that. And for bridges you need pontoon boats to string across the river and planks to nail on."

"So was your brother with you?" I asked. "Was he in the Union army, too? We were wondering about that."

"Well, of course he was," the ghost said. "What do you think I was doing there except trying to take care of him?"

"We just figured you both joined up together," Greg said. "At least that's what I thought. I read last night that they would take guys even if they were teenagers, and some were really young teenagers and lied about their age."

"I didn't lie about my age," the ghost said. "Or Frankie's, either. Might have fudged a little, okay, but a lie — that's when you're trying to pull one over on somebody and do something mean to them, and we didn't do anything mean to anybody. We just joined up was all. And thank you for the bonus money, too."

I wanted to ask a hundred more questions, but Julie beat me to it. "Can you tell us anything else about that day, December 6, and the scouting party you were on?"

"Saw more Johnny Rebs," he said. "I remember that. Frankie was nervous, but I reminded him about us shouting over to the Rebs the day before and them shouting back, and us having a pretty regular conversation. Then I pulled out a sack of sugar and showed it to him. He asked me what it was for and I said it was for trading with the Rebels, of course."

"How did you trade it?" Julie asked.

"Went out on the rocks as far as I could get. Me and another fellow from my unit. Couple of those Rebels did the same. We probably weren't more than twenty feet apart from them, but couldn't get close, so we had to hurl that sack to them and they had to hurl back what they had for us."

"Tobacco?" Julie asked.

The ghost nodded.

"You know that's bad for you, don't you?" Julie asked. "It can give you cancer."

The ghost blinked at her the way he'd done the day before when we made reference to things that were totally foreign to him. Then he shrugged. "Doesn't much matter, 'cause they caught the bag of sugar, but they couldn't get enough throw into that tobacco pouch and it landed square in the water. I thought my buddy was going to jump right in after it, but I held him back. Wasn't a thing we could do about it except stand there and try not to cry."

"So you didn't get anything in the trade?" Greg asked.

The ghost shook his head. "Not that day. They said if we came back the next day, they'd have some more for us, though, so we said okay, we would volunteer again for scout duty. It wasn't until about then that I saw those Rebels we'd been trading with, a couple of them didn't have shoes or boots on, just rags tied around their feet. Those boys were cold and shivering a whole lot worse than us. I mean, I couldn't feel my toes, but at least I had leather boots on."

"Is there anything else you remember about that day?" Julie asked. "Anything else about your brother or your unit, besides your brother's name?"

The ghost went back into blinking mode for a minute, and then shook his head. "Frankie was real quiet anyway, and he didn't say much. I made sure he stayed on the driest ground anywhere we went, and I made him stay to the back, away from the riverbank, just in case there were some of those Rebels over there who had a big idea to shoot at us instead of trade with us. But that didn't happen. Didn't happen on that day anyway."

He blinked some more, not saying anything else, and I hoped there might be more. There was.

"Oh yeah," he continued. "When we came back, those pontoons were still just sitting there where they'd been since the end of November. Some of them had come from Washington, some on wagons a hundred miles all the way from Harper's Ferry. They were parked up on the ridge high above the Rappahannock River. We had artillery up there and had been shelling the town off and on — any time any of their snipers decided to take potshots at us. Now the engineers — that's the boys who had the job of putting together the bridges — they just needed to find a way to get the pontoons down to the river, and into the river, and across the river, and you could just tell that wasn't going to be easy. Not easy at all."

The way the ghost had settled in, just chattering away about the events of December 6, 1862, had me thinking he would just stick around and keep talking for the rest of the afternoon. I had been trying to figure out his accent since the day before, and the whole time he talked today I kept trying. I finally decided it must be a New York accent, though not a very strong one. There was a kind of musical quality to his voice, too, that I still couldn't quite figure out.

Then, before I could, and almost right in the middle of a sentence, the ghost vanished. He knew it as it was happening, because he even managed to blurt out, "Wait!"

And just like that he was gone.

"Wow!" Greg said. "That was fast."

"I know," Julie said. "Usually it's more gradual than that. That made me dizzy."

"Me too," Greg said, and he put his hands on his beanie as if to stop his head from spinning. I was pretty sure he was just playing along with Julie, not that she seemed to mind. She smiled at him and he smiled back at her.

"It didn't make me dizzy," I said, partly just to be contrary. "Just frustrated. We still didn't find out his name, or what regiment or brigade or anything he was in, or where he was from, though I'm guessing it's New York."

Julie nodded. I guess she wasn't dizzy anymore. "I was thinking that, too. Because of his accent."

"I kind of thought he might be Irish," Greg said. "Or part Irish anyway."

"That's it!" I exclaimed. "That's the musical part of his voice I couldn't figure out. He's New Yorkish *and* he's Irish."

"I don't think New Yorkish is a word," Julie said, but I let it go. She knew what I meant. Greg nodded in agreement.

"Yeah, that sounds about right," he said. "Now we just need him to come back so we can ask him. Maybe us suggesting it will help him remember."

"Wonder if he'll come back today?" I asked. As if in answer, the hounds on the other side of the wall at the Dog and Suds started howling.

"Probably not," Julie said. "So maybe we should actually do something with these instruments."

"Like what?" Greg asked.

Julie rolled her eyes. "Uh, like practice?"

CHAPTER 10

Belman — not Little Belman, but the real Belman — was back giving us a hard time the next day at school. He came up behind us in the cafeteria and didn't say anything at first. Julie had something called a bento box that her dad, who was Japanese, had made for her, with Japanese food: sushi, edamame, and seaweed salad. (Julie's mom was American, and when she made Julie's lunch it was usually just a peanut butter sandwich.) Belman grabbed a piece of sushi, lifted the top slice of bread off Greg's peanut butter sandwich, and shoved the sushi down on the peanut butter. Then he smashed the bread back on top. He started to do something with Julie's seaweed salad, but she pinched the back of his hand with her chopsticks and that stopped him.

"Hey, I was just going to look at it," Belman said. "I never saw anybody eat grass before. I thought only cows did that."

"It's not grass," Julie said. "Now leave us alone."

Belman pretended to have his feelings hurt. "Ouch! Here I am just trying to be friendly and you're being rude to me. That's not nice."

"You're not nice," Greg said, examining his sandwich and probably trying to decide if it would still be edible if he took the sushi off.

Belman's voice changed, and so did the look on his face. "You're right," he said. "I'm not. Especially when some little punks go scaring my sister. We look out for one another in my family, so you three better watch out."

He didn't wait for us to respond. Instead he grabbed Greg's peanut butter sandwich — with the sushi still inside — and ate it. Then he left.

"I'm beginning to not like that guy," Greg said, which was the understatement of the day.

•   •   •

That afternoon at band practice we had just worked our way through one song when Julie stopped playing, right in the middle of the chorus.

"What?" Greg asked. "Why'd you stop playing?"

"Because I've been thinking about something," she said. "About the ghost."

Greg and I waited, still holding our guitar picks above the strings as if Julie might decide instead to finish the song. She didn't.

"Well, ever since Little Belman said the ghost was a girl, I keep picturing his face and just, well, wondering."

"You mean if he could actually be a girl?" I asked.

"Yes," she said. "I mean no. I mean I'm not sure. He's so young, for one thing. And you can tell he doesn't shave. There's no beard or anything, or even, like, the stubble of a beard. Or peach fuzz. And remember how when we first saw him I said 'she' instead of 'he,' but I didn't even realize it at first? Maybe I subconsciously recognized that the ghost was a girl even then."

"That could be," Greg said. "And another thing — we were talking about how the ghost had a New York accent and maybe an Irish accent, but did you guys notice he also has a pretty high voice, kind of like a girl's?"

"This is crazy," I said, even though I had noticed that, too. "Why would a girl be in the army? And pretending to be a boy?"

Greg drummed his fingers on his guitar for a second. "They let women in the army now," he said.

"Yeah," I countered. "But they didn't let them in back then."

"About that," Julie said, "I've been doing some research."

"And what did you find out?" I asked.

"That there were actually hundreds of women who fought in the Union and the Confederate armies during the Civil War. They dressed up like men, in uniforms, and just pretended they were guys."

"Wow," Greg said. "That *is* crazy. Why would they do that?"

"All kinds of reasons," Julie said. "Maybe they wanted to serve with a family member, or even their husband, or maybe they just believed in the cause they were fighting for so much that they wanted to be part of the fight, or maybe for a lot of them it was for the money. There were a lot of really poor people back then, and women didn't have a lot of options for jobs that paid very much."

"But how could they get away with it?" I asked.

"From what I read, it wasn't very hard," Julie said. "They'd cut their hair short, and uniforms usually didn't fit too well so they'd get a loose-fitting uniform. And a lot of times when you joined the army they didn't have a doctor examine you, they just maybe looked at your teeth and made sure you had two arms and two legs and the right number of fingers and toes, and made sure you could see okay, and that you weren't too obviously sick, and that was the end of it. So nobody ever saw you with your clothes off."

"What about when you took a shower, or went to the bathroom?" Greg asked. "That must have been weird."

"Not really," Julie said. "Back then they hardly ever took baths or showered or anything. They slept in their uniforms. And if you went to the bathroom you could just go out in the woods and do your business and nobody had to see you. It just wasn't that hard to pull off pretending you were a man. Or a teenage boy."

"So are you saying that our ghost was — is — actually a girl?" I asked.

Julie shrugged. "I don't know. I'm just saying that Little Belman got me wondering if it's possible, that's all."

"Well, anything's possible," I said, though I still wasn't buying the idea.

"Did you find out anything else in your research about this?" Greg asked, not ready to quit the topic.

Julie nodded. "Here's the totally crazy part. There were at least three women that they know about who fought in the Battle of Fredericksburg. One was a girl, a teenager, named Lizzie Compton. She had joined the army — pretending to be a boy — when she was just thirteen or fourteen, and she fought in a bunch of battles, on the Union side. She got wounded during the Battle of Fredericksburg but recovered. That's how they found out she was a girl — when the doctors were treating her and bandaging up her wounds."

"What did they do then?" Greg asked.

"Made her leave the army," Julie said, "but apparently she just joined up again under a different name and fought with another unit."

Greg grinned. "That's awesome."

"And there was another woman, a lady named Sarah Edmonds," Julie continued. "She used the fake name of Private Franklin Thompson, and during the Battle of Fredericksburg she was an orderly, and she rode a horse for twelve straight hours the day of the battle, under fire just about the whole time, bringing orders and reports from the headquarters to the front and back."

"What about the others?" Greg asked. I was too dumb-founded by all Julie was saying to ask any questions myself.

"The third woman who fought on the Union side, they just knew she was from New Jersey, and she was a corporal at the start of the battle, but she was so fierce and heroic in battle that they promoted her to sergeant. And that's not all."

Greg and I were both just sitting there openmouthed, stunned by all Julie was telling us.

"It turned out that during the battle she was pregnant!" Julie exclaimed. "And a month later — just one month later! — she had a baby."

That was so wild that Greg and I had to laugh and shake our heads. "You swear you're not making this up?" Greg asked.

Julie raised her right hand. "I totally swear. And that lady Sarah Edmonds, she actually wrote a book that was sort of about her experiences in the war. In her book — which was a bestseller right after the war — she pretended that she had just been a nurse and a spy during the war, but stuff came out later that people knew about her actually being in uniform during the fighting and pretending to be a man."

"So it's definitely possible that our ghost is a girl!" I said, still not believing that I was saying such a thing. But the more Julie talked, and the more I pictured our ghost, and the more I thought about her voice and the way she looked, and how certain Little Belman was, the more I was starting to come around.

The dogs next door got louder again with their barking and we all looked over at the wall.

"This would be the perfect time for the ghost to show up," Greg said. "You know, we're talking about him and zeroing in on this big question, and then, boom, dogs start barking and then he shows up and remembers everything."

"Just like in the movies," Julie said.

"What movies?" Greg asked.

Julie sighed. "It's just an expression, Greg. You know how movies always end in clichés. Coincidences happen. That sort of thing."

"Well, this isn't exactly a movie," I said.

The ghost must have agreed, because he — or possibly she — didn't show up that afternoon. We stumbled through a couple of songs and then we all went upstairs to head for home.

CHAPTER 11

As we rode our bikes down Hanover Street, shivering from the cold, Julie said, "During the Civil War everything in front of us was open fields." Now it was a neighborhood full of houses and streets. The high school football stadium was at the bottom of the long hill we were coasting down. Julie continued, "So basically once the Union troops started down this hill there was no cover." She pointed ahead of us, where the land and the street rose up again, higher than the hill we were on. "Marye's Heights was where the Confederates held the high ground with their headquarters and their artillery, and all their troops, or half of them, actually, dug in behind the stone wall at Sunken Road."

We all knew the stone wall and Sunken Road because the battlefield there was a national park, and tourists came all the time to walk around and see where the Battle of Fredericksburg took place. I tried to imagine what it looked like back in 1862 — to the Union soldiers having to go down this hill and then cross open fields to attack the Confederates, and to the Confederate troops opposite them, dug in behind that stone wall, looking down on the tens of thousands of soldiers in blue, exposed as they marched forward toward the Rebel positions, bayonets attached to the ends of their muskets, cannonballs flying back and forth between the two great armies, and a cold winter sun.

We all stopped our bikes halfway down the hill to zip up our jackets. Maybe they were thinking, and seeing, the same thing I was. Everything felt ghostly to me all of a sudden as I thought about the thousands of men — and some girls and women pretending to be men — who fought here, right exactly here, and so many of them died here in the most terrible ways.

"Well, bye, you guys," I finally said, my voice faint for some reason, as I started up again and coasted to the bottom of the hill. They kept going straight, in the direction of Sunken Road — Greg said he was going to ride with Julie the rest of the way to her house since it was getting dark. I turned right on Kenmore Avenue. As I headed west to my neighborhood I remembered something else we'd read — that Kenmore actually used to be a stream — they called it a millrace because it carried water over from the river to operate a mill there south of town — and it was one more obstacle the Union soldiers had to get past on their march to their doom.

·   ·   ·

My mind was churning with all the questions we had, and how few answers, when I got home. Mom was just texting me, wondering where I was and to tell me dinner was on the table, when I walked in.

"You know the days are getting shorter," she said, her voice sharper than it had been in the hospital. "We were starting to get worried."

Dad brought in the food from the kitchen and put it on the dining room table. "You know the rule, Anderson," he said. "Always call or text if you're going to be late."

"I'm sorry," I said. "We just got caught up in practice and stuff."

Mom managed to smile, but only barely, and I realized she was still in some pain, either from the MS or from the fall. I felt even worse then about being late and making her worry. I went over and gave her a big hug, and for some reason we both just stayed there for, like, a whole minute or more, hugging each other.

"Hey," Dad said finally. "Dinner's getting cold and you're leaving me out!"

Instead of us stopping hugging to eat, though, we let Dad come over and join us and we had one of those big dorky group hugs people always make fun of but that sure felt good right then and there. Sometimes, for no good reason, you just want to be that close to your mom and dad, and you almost feel like you could hold on to them like that the whole rest of the night.

·   ·   ·

Julie texted me and Greg later, after dinner. *Hey you guys. Did you know today is Pearl Harbor Day?*

She didn't text anything else, but I knew what she was thinking — or rather who she was thinking about: our first ghost, William Foxwell, who was in the Navy in World War II and served on an aircraft carrier called the *Yorktown* until he went missing during the famous Battle of Midway in the middle of the Pacific Ocean. We helped him remember what happened — how he went missing and how he died — so he could finally find peace all these years later.

The war started for him, as it did with the rest of America, with the Japanese sneak attack on Pearl Harbor in Hawaii on December 7, 1941.

I texted Julie and Greg back — *We shouldn't ever forget* — and then said a prayer for our friend.

I slept fitfully that night, tossing and turning and once nearly falling out of bed from flopping around so much. I woke up and found myself hanging off the edge with the covers twisted up around my legs. I was shivering, too. It took me a couple of minutes to untwist the sheets and blankets and set everything back in order so I could crawl back under and not be freezing. My mind was still busy, though — first from dreams about ghosts, and then from all those questions I'd come home with about our newest ghost. In my dreams, all the ghosts we'd met so far were singing "The Battle Hymn of the Republic," which was, of course, really weird. And then I couldn't get it out of my head.

I wished our new ghost would show up in my room like the other three had done, but I didn't expect it to happen for some reason. Things just seemed different about our Civil

War ghost. He was okay coming next door from the Dog and Suds to the Kitchen Sink basement, but that was about all. And where had he been today? Had he been close enough to hear us talking — and speculating on the possibility that he was a girl in disguise? — but not close enough for us to see him?

At some point in the night I did the mental math and figured out we were just six days away from the anniversary of the actual Battle of Fredericksburg — December 13. And if we weren't able to figure out what happened to our ghost by then, I wondered if that would be it, if our chance would be gone, and if the ghost would be stuck haunting the Dog and Suds forever, every year from the middle of November until the middle of December. Would we have to wait until next year to try again? Would he even come back next year?

I wished the rules for ghosts were more consistent, and made more sense, but every time seemed to be another wild ride, no matter how much we thought we had this stuff figured out.

. . .

The next day didn't start off very well. Somebody — and we knew it must have been Belman — had superglued the locks on our lockers so we couldn't get in to get our books that morning. The janitor had to come in with bolt cutters and cut all our locks. Julie told the principal we were sure it was Belman, but when they called him down to the office Belman denied everything, of course. Any time the principal wasn't looking, Belman smirked at me and Greg and Julie, so much so that I thought Greg was going to explode. Julie kept hold of his left arm and I kept hold of his right.

After Belman left, the principal made us stay. "Without any evidence, there's nothing more I can do here," he said.

"You can search his locker for superglue!" Greg said, louder than he should have.

The principal looked annoyed. "The janitor already did that," he said. "We'll be keeping an eye on things. Not only on Mr. Belman, but on the three of you, too. I have to wonder what might have happened to provoke something like this." He stared at us for a second with this accusing look on his face, until I actually started feeling kind of guilty.

"You'll need to purchase new combination locks for your lockers," the principal said. "We can't replace those for you. Be sure to register the combination in the office when you bring those in."

Then he dismissed us. We were barely out in the hall before Greg launched into how unfair the whole thing was, and how he was really going to get back at Belman this time, and how —

But Julie cut him off. "No," she said. "We can't keep doing things to get back at him, or his sister, or anyone. All that does is escalate things."

"So what are we supposed to do?" I asked. "Turn the other cheek?"

Greg sniffed. "The other butt cheek maybe."

"Just let it go for now," Julie said. "We have more important things. And to be fair to Belman, we did frighten his little sister half to death."

"Not we," I said. "The ghost."

Julie shrugged. "Pretty much the same thing."

Greg sniffed again. "Don't forget how she got back at us with those water balloons," he said.

I shook my head. "I'm beginning to understand a little bit more about how all these wars get started," I said, and that was the end of it. We hurried off to our classes and had to carry all our books and notebooks and everything else from our lockers with us the whole day long. By seventh period I was exhausted.

CHAPTER 12

During study hall I went to the library to research more about the Battle of Fredericksburg. Though we'd learned about it in school, and though Uncle Dex and Julie had confirmed it, that whole business about the Union army having to wait weeks for pontoons to arrive so they could cross the Rappahannock just didn't make sense. How could such a huge plan with that many soldiers and generals and logistics get so messed up, and by something so simple? But the more I read, the more I could see how it happened. Everybody seemed to blame the guy in Washington, DC, who was in charge of the supplies — he was called the quartermaster — for not moving quickly enough, but I guess he did try. He had to get most of the pontoons all the way from Harpers Ferry, West Virginia, although it wasn't West Virginia yet. It was still part of Virginia, and didn't break off from the rest of Virginia until June 1863, as it turned out, because the people in those Virginia counties voted themselves out of the Confederacy and into the Union — so, no longer part of Virginia.

Boy, the things you learned on the way to learning about other things!

Anyway, roads were terrible so it was impossible to transport the pontoons that way. They tried floating some down the Potomac River, but it wasn't enough. They needed hundreds of pontoons, and they weighed, like, a ton each, just like Julie had said, and they got started late, and they didn't have enough pontoons so had to order more built. And on and on went the problems.

And meanwhile, just like the ghost said, the 130,000 Union soldiers just sat around and waited. And waited. And waited. They marched drills. Scrounged around for any local food to eat. Some of them were sent out on scouting parties, though they were never able to find anywhere else to cross the river except right there in Fredericksburg. Everywhere else was too difficult to get to, or too rocky to cross, or they thought it was already defended by the Confederates.

Meanwhile, Confederate snipers hiding out on the Fredericksburg side of the river shot at the Union guards on the Stafford side of the river until one of the Union generals sent a message over to the mayor of Fredericksburg that if the citizens didn't stop providing hiding places for the Rebels, then the Union cannons would bomb the city.

The snipers quit sniping.

I also found out something else during study hall. The Union army had lost one battle after another after another through much of the first two years of the Civil War, suffering a lot more casualties than the Confederates. People in the North were getting angry and frustrated, and a lot of them were calling for an end to the war. President Lincoln knew he couldn't quit, though. The cause was too important. He had issued an Emancipation Proclamation declaring that on January 1, 1863, all the slaves in the Confederate states would be free, and he was convinced that for people to believe it would make any difference, the Union needed a victory — and a big one at that — just before he did it.

I was the first one to band practice that afternoon — or at least I thought I was. Uncle Dex told me on my way in that Julie and Greg weren't there yet. He had his new music system set up and was playing old rock albums. The one he had on when I walked through was a band called The Band, which was pretty weird. The song was weird, too. Uncle Dex said it was called "The Night They Drove Old Dixie Down." I stood and listened for a couple of minutes. I liked the song, but more than that I was knocked out that a seventies rock band would write about the Civil War.

As I headed downstairs to our practice room, I heard voices. And not just any voices, either. I recognized them right away: Little Belman and our ghost. And they were arguing. They didn't even notice me when I walked in, so I stood there just inside the door and listened.

"I know you're a girl," Little Belman insisted.

The ghost — on the other side of the room from Little Belman — snapped. "I already told you, ain't none of your business who I am. I can out-shoot, out-march, and out-fight just about anybody in President Lincoln's army. Out-ride, too, if I only had a horse, which I don't. Not that that's none of your business, neither. Now why don't you run on along and go play with baby dolls or something. Your mama's probably out looking for you to change your diaper."

"I don't wear diapers," Little Belman snapped right back. "I'm in fifth grade and I'm not leaving until you tell the truth. You're a *girl*!"

"And if I wasn't all the way over here, I'd come over there and give you a good whooping," the ghost said. At first I thought he meant if he wasn't all the way across the room from Little Belman, but then I realized it was a different kind of distance he was talking about, the kind between the living and the dead, or the mostly dead, or whatever these ghosts were.

"You don't scare me," Little Belman said.

The ghost took what was probably meant to be a menacing step forward toward Little Belman, but I decided it was time for me to intervene.

"How did you get in here?" I demanded.

Little Belman whirled around. "Where did you come from?"

I had to laugh. "You're standing here talking to a ghost and you want to know where *I* came from? *I* came from upstairs."

Little Belman glared at me. "Well, *I* snuck in when that man up there had his back turned."

I put my hands on my hips and stood up as tall as I could and tried to sound like a grown-up. "Well, you better leave right now, because you don't have permission to be here, and I'd hate to have to call your mom and tell her about you trespassing on private property."

Little Belman put her hands on her hips, too. "I'll tell her about the ghost," she said.

"She won't believe you," I said back. "Nobody will."

"My brother will," she said, though I could see the doubt in her eyes.

"Anyway, what ghost are you talking about?" I asked, looking around, pretending there was nobody — or nothing — there, which was easy, because the ghost had disappeared shortly after I interrupted their argument.

Little Belman looked around, too. She even raced around the room looking high and low, though there really wasn't anywhere for the ghost or anybody else to hide, if that's what they wanted to do. She stopped at the mysterious trunk. It was closed up tight, though, and she didn't try to open it. I wondered what had drawn her there, though. And I wondered how it was that she could see, and talk to, the ghost. And why she was so convinced that the ghost was a girl — not that Julie didn't have me and Greg wondering the same thing.

"All right," Little Belman announced. "I'm leaving. But don't think for a minute that this is over."

"Whatever," I said. "Just be careful on the stairs."

She stuck out her tongue at me and turned around to leave. I heard her stomping the whole way — just like a little kid.

CHAPTER 13

Once again, Julie and Greg came in right after Little Belman left.

"Here again?" Julie asked. "Really?"

"Yeah," I said. "She said she snuck in and I believe her."

"She nearly stomped on my foot as she stomped out of the store," Greg said. "Your uncle was singing along to a Led Zeppelin song — 'When the Levee Breaks' — and you know what she said to him, just before she stormed out?"

I shrugged.

"She said, 'Your hippie music gives me a headache,'" Greg said.

"Wow!" I said. "How rude."

"I know," Greg said. "That's just what I said to Julie."

Julie nodded. "It's true. That's exactly what he said. Although I have to say I kind of agree with the Little Belman."

I was still stuck on the fact that Greg knew what Led Zeppelin song was playing. And as if to emphasize the point, he picked up his guitar, plugged it in, turned on his amp, and started cranking through what appeared to be the chords for that levee song he mentioned. He sang some of it, too, his voice cracking, until Julie shushed him.

"I think Anderson has heard enough," she said, as if I was the one stopping him.

The ghost — who had a really bad habit of just suddenly showing up and suddenly disappearing, with hardly ever any gentle fading in or out — just then popped into the room.

"Hate the voice, but kind of like the song," he said to Greg, as if he'd been in the conversation all along.

"Thanks," Greg said. "I guess."

I said welcome back to the ghost, and thought about filling Julie and Greg in on Little Belman interrogating the ghost and insisting he was a girl, but then it occurred to me that the whole girl business wasn't something the ghost wanted me to talk about. So I switched directions and asked the ghost if he remembered anything else since the last time we saw him, which was two days before.

"What day is it today," he answered. "I mean the date and all."

"December 8," Julie said.

The ghost nodded. "Still cold," he said. "Still snow on the ground. Couldn't nobody hardly sleep at night. Kept big fires burning all the time. Had fellows up all night on fire watch to make sure they kept blazing. We probably burned down a whole couple of forests those weeks we were in Virginia. I shared my blanket with Frankie. Nothing special about that. Anybody would do the same. I already told you how Mama and Papa made me swear I would always take care of Frankie, and I tried to never let them down or let Frankie down."

I wasn't sure the ghost had actually ever told us that before, but I didn't interrupt because I wanted him to keep going. He seemed to be on a roll.

"Another day, another scout party down to the river," he continued. "Same area as before, and some of those same Johnny Rebs as before on their side of the river. They hailed us and we hailed them right back, and we were negotiating another trade. But then right smack in the middle of it there was a rifle went off somewhere above us, and then another, and then a dozen more, and three of those Rebel boys fell into the river and the others took off running back into the trees. It was another one of our scout parties, with a lieutenant who hated Rebels and didn't believe any of us should be friendly to any of them."

He went silent for a minute, then started up again. "That lieutenant, he came down with his men and hollered at us good and proper, said we could get a court-martial for what he called 'fraternizing with the enemy,' which is just a fancy way of saying we didn't try to kill them the second we saw them. Now I'm not saying I was going soft, or that anybody on that scout party I was on was going soft. Maybe Frankie a little bit, but he always had a sensitive nature, and he played banjo at the campfires at nights and that kept everybody's spirits up and that's a mighty valuable service if I do say so myself."

"Music is important," Greg said, which sounded kind of dumb, but seemed to cheer up the ghost.

"Darn right it is," he said. "So anyway, I was just about to feel sorry for those dead Rebs — there one minute talking to us about wishing they had boots like ours instead of rags tied on their feet, and then the next minute dead and done, and their bodies washing away downriver."

"What do you mean you were just about to feel sorry for them?" Greg asked. He seemed to be our spokesman for the day.

"Just what I said," the ghost said. "But then there was rustling in the woods across the river and we all dropped behind river rocks and aimed our muskets, but who came out of the woods wasn't Johnny Rebs but Negroes, some men, some women, some children."

"Were they slaves?" I asked. "Escaping?"

The ghost nodded. "That's what we found out once we got them across. Some were carrying bundles on their heads half as big as themselves, and I was afraid they might fall in, so we dashed out on the rocks — which was foolish, as there could have been Rebel snipers in the woods opposite us — and helped them over. One of our big fellows picked up one little boy and one little girl and tucked one under each arm and carried them across, hopping rock to rock, that way."

"I read that a number of slaves escaped from Fredericksburg during the battle and even more when the Union army finally captured the city," Julie said.

"All I know is we passed them along to the other scout party and they escorted the slave families on up to Falmouth, and who knows where else from there."

"To freedom," Greg said solemnly.

"Sounds about right," the ghost said. "Or maybe Washington, DC."

"I read that there were half a million slaves in Virginia at the start of the war," Julie said. "And Virginia had the largest slave population of any of the southern states."

The ghost shrugged. "I don't know nothing about that," he said. "I know this one slave woman told us they sent a lot of the men slaves down to Richmond and made them work in the factories making cannons and such. And had them building up the defenses around their capital, too, doing most of the labor. Those Confederates were bound and determined to get every last ounce of work out of their slaves while they still had them, I guess. That woman also told us that at a lot of the farms and plantations around Fredericksburg, it was women and their children doing most of the farm work 'cause the Rebels took so many of the slave men and put them hard at work for the war."

"Boy," I said. "How ironic is that? Making the slaves work to basically keep them as slaves."

The ghost scratched his head. "I think I follow you there. Well, anyway, we confiscated them like we were ordered to."

"Huh?" said Greg. "Confiscated?"

"The slaves," the ghost said. "That was the law. We were supposed to declare that they were contraband of war and confiscate them. On account of they were property of the Confederates, and any property aiding the Rebels' war effort that we captured, we kept and passed on up the line. Then once we confiscated them I guess then they got to be free. I don't exactly know about that. I just know seeing the faces of those folks crossing that river, it made me remember what the fight was all about, and it wasn't just us killing Johnny Rebs, even though that's what it felt like sometimes. That slave woman, you could just tell in her face how sad she was that they sent those men in her family, her husband, I guess, away so she might never see him again. Those children with her, you could see it in their faces, too. And they were scared to death. Somebody said they were scared we would send them back across the river and they'd get beat or worse for running away."

I thought about that old slave auction block that sat on a corner downtown, on William Street. It was where they used to do actual slave auctions, but even with a plaque there explaining all that, tourists would still have their kids stand on top of the auction block and pose for pictures. How awful it must have been for those slaves, and the families of those slaves, to have their parents or their children or their friends sold and sent away — forever. I got really sad thinking about it. And glad that our ghost had fought on the right side of the war.

The ghost had been just standing there for a minute, stroking his chin, thinking hard. Then he picked back up where he'd left off. "I still felt bad about the ambush of those Rebels we'd been talking to before that at the river," he said. "But after seeing those runaway slaves, I didn't feel quite as bad, knowing what those boys were fighting for and remembering what we were fighting against."

The ghost left shortly after

that. I never did bring up the conversation he'd been having with Little Belman, but I told Julie and Greg about it once the ghost was gone.

"That Little Belman is so rude," Greg said when I finished. "What a little meanie."

"She really is just like her brother," Julie said.

They spent the next few minutes discussing the Belmans while I thought back through the conversation I'd overheard. There was something there I had missed, I just felt it, but I couldn't think what it could be. Maybe something the ghost said. Or maybe something the ghost didn't say.

And then it hit me. "You guys!" I said. "I just remembered. When Little Belman was asking the ghost about being a girl, the ghost kept saying how he could out-fight and out-march and out-shoot any soldier in the Union army, but he didn't ever actually just come right out and deny that he was a girl."

Greg and Julie stared at me for a second, and then Greg asked, "And he never said anything like 'I am a boy'?"

"Or 'I am a man'?" Julie added.

"Right," I said. "I mean, neither one. He didn't say he wasn't a girl, and he didn't say he was a boy. Just all that other stuff. And Little Belman kept saying over and over that she knew the ghost was a girl. You'd think the ghost would get mad about it. Well, I guess he did get mad about it, but not scary-ghost mad. More like defensive-ghost mad, now that I think about it."

"Curiouser and curiouser," Julie said.

Greg gave her a quizzical look.

"It's from *Alice in Wonderland*," Julie said. "Alice says it when she turns into a giant."

"Oh," said Greg. "I never read that."

"You really should sometime," Julie said.

"Guys!" I snapped. "Can we focus here? I'm just about convinced that our ghost soldier is a girl."

Julie shrugged. "I was already convinced," she said.

Greg nodded. "Maybe if we ask him about it — in a nice way, that doesn't make him defensive and angry — then it will help him, or her, remember his, or her, name. And what unit he, or she, was with in the Union army. And who his, or her, brother was. And where they were from. And why she pretended to be a boy and join the army? And what happened to her, or him, or whoever?"

The pronoun uncertainty was driving me crazy. Greg, too, apparently, because he started rubbing his temples as if he had a headache. Come to think of it, I had a headache, too.

"Good points," Julie said. "But he's gone now, and he doesn't seem to be showing up very often."

"Yeah," said Greg, still rubbing his head. "Just pops in, stays for a while, tells us what happened on this particular date in 1862, then pops back out into the whatever."

"Into limbo?" Julie suggested.

"Yeah," said Greg. "I guess so. And, you know, also next door into the Dog and Suds."

The dogs had started barking again and we could, of course, hear them all too loud and all too clear through the basement wall.

"I think maybe we should call off practice today," Greg said. "My head hurts, and now with those dogs going crazy it hurts even more."

"Want me to ride with you to your house?" Julie asked. "Just to make sure you can get home okay?"

Greg blushed but said sure. Neither of them looked at me. I just rolled my eyes at how weird they were being.

"You guys go on ahead," I said. "I have to do a couple of things here and then I'll head home after that."

They didn't even bother to ask me what I needed to do. They just grabbed their stuff and said good-bye and left.

I sat and waited until I was sure they were gone, and until Uncle Dex hollered downstairs that he was closing up shop and would I please make sure the front door was locked behind me when I took off, too?

I assured him that I would. I didn't actually have anything I had to do in the basement, though I did pick up my guitar and played some. I tried picking out the melodies of some of our songs, but I wasn't nearly as good at that as

Greg, so I switched back to just playing chords. Next thing I knew I wasn't playing any of our songs. I was playing "The Battle Hymn of the Republic," and thinking about all the ghosts singing it in that dream I had. I started singing along, softly:

Mine eyes have seen the glory of the coming of the Lord;
He is trampling out the vintage where the grapes of wrath
*   are stored;*
He hath loosed the fateful lightning of His terrible swift
*   sword:*
His truth is marching on.

I knew it had been written during the Civil War, but I wondered if the ghost had ever heard it, or if it came later, after the ghost turned into a ghost.

I didn't have to wonder long, though, because pretty soon another high voice joined in with mine for the "Glory, glory, hallelujahs," and there was the ghost, standing next to me, singing along.

I didn't know any other verses, so just listened as the ghost kept singing and I kept playing my guitar:

I have seen Him in the watch-fires of a hundred
   circling camps,
They have builded Him an altar in the evening dews
   and damps;
I can read His righteous sentence by the dim and
   flaring lamps:
His day is marching on.

Performing with a ghost from the Civil War! I had to figure it was about the coolest thing ever. There seemed to be a million more verses — well, four, anyway — and the ghost knew them all, and he kept singing in that high, and, well, pretty voice all the way to the final "Glory, glory, hallelujah," and the last "While God is marching on."

We both sat quietly for a few minutes once it was over, and it seemed to me there was a sweet echo of our voices reverberating through the room. I didn't hear it so much as I felt it, and I wondered if the ghost did, too. I kind of thought so.

Finally, the ghost spoke.

"I know why you stuck around here," he said. "After your gang left."

"Uh, you do?" I said.

He nodded. "You heard what that little girl said and you got to wondering about it, too. Was I a girl."

"Well, yeah," I said. "Sort of. I mean, it did come up when we were talking earlier this week — me and Julie and Greg. My, uh, gang. But I wasn't going to say anything. I don't want to be rude or anything."

The ghost sighed. "I guess it ain't rude to wonder. And once that little girl got going about it, it got *me* wondering about it, too. I don't know how that girl saw what she did. I have to give it to her, though — she may be meaner than a snake, but she's a tough little thing. Wouldn't have minded having her with us in President Lincoln's army. She'd have whipped up on her share of Rebels, and then some."

I thought about it and had to agree. "I bet she would," I said.

Then I waited some more. The ghost got up and paced around the room for a few minutes, not saying anything, at least not to me, but he seemed to be muttering to himself, too low for me to hear exactly what.

And then he stopped and turned to me. "I remember now." He swallowed hard.

"In the uniform like you see me right now, my name is Sam, only they call me Sammy."

He swallowed hard again. "But inside the uniform, I ain't a Sam or a Sammy neither one."

The ghost sat down again. At first I thought this was all too hard for him and he might even start crying. But then a sort of sly grin appeared on his face.

"Nope," he said. "Not Sam or Sammy."

The grin spread even wider.

"Might as well tell you, I'm a girl all right, just like she said, and my real name is Sally."

CHAPTER 15

Telling me she was a girl, something she'd kept secret from the world for more than a hundred and fifty years, seemed to be an enormous relief for Sally. Suddenly, she remembered a lot more about her past, and the story came pouring out as we sat together in the Kitchen Sink basement. The dogs next door went totally quiet, as if they were straining to listen in.

"I already told you about Mama and Papa," Sally said. "How the consumption took them both. There's too much grief in my heart for me to talk any more about the particulars of when they passed. I was with them both times, at the sanatorium. I made Frankie wait outside. Where we were living then was upstate New York, in Schenectady, and had dairy cows. Me and Frankie milked them every day and night, and Mama taught us to make the soft and hard cheeses. You name it. Hard work, but I guess we did all right. Frankie and me got to go to school most days, although some days the chores were too much and kept us away."

She paused for a second, and then said softly, "We lost the farm once Mama and Papa died. I was fifteen and Frankie was fourteen."

"What did you do then?" I asked. "Did you have other family you could live with?"

She shook her head. "And weren't a lot of people wanted to take in Irish kids. They thought we'd be trouble. So Mrs. Slominsky — she was the teacher at our school — she gave us the name of a cousin of hers in New York City, said her cousin could help me get on at a clothing factory, and point us to where we could live. And that's what happened. Frankie got a job working with a street vendor, but I didn't like him being out there all day without me. Things could happen in the city, and they did. Twice he got beat up for being Irish and wandering into the wrong neighborhood. I don't know why those city toughs hated the Irish so much but they did, a lot of them. Anybody say anything to me and I'd give 'em a black eye, but Frankie wasn't any kind of a fighter.

"But it was still a good thing he had any kind of work. It gave him something to do, someplace to be. The flophouse we stayed at turned us out at the crack of dawn and wouldn't let us back in until sundown, so we had to have something to keep Frankie occupied while I was at the factory. I hated that sewing, though. I could do it okay, don't get me wrong about that. I might be a tomboy, but I know plenty of girl things. My mama saw to that. But Papa needed me to work a man's job on the farm and that's what I did. He expected the same out of Frankie, but Frankie's always been more delicate, you might say, so I always did half of his chores after I did mine."

I tried to imagine what it must have been like for Sally and Frankie so long ago, having to make it on their own without their parents. Just losing their parents must have been so devastating. I worried all the time about my mom with her MS, and what would happen if — I guess when — it got a lot worse. I couldn't even bring myself to think about not having my mom around.

And then to have to fend for yourselves — and in Sally's case, to move from the town you grew up in, and make your way in a big city, and work all day and sleep in a flophouse at night — just seemed like too much for anybody to have to manage. Sally said her workday was ten hours long, and sometimes twelve. And they didn't get to take breaks at all, except for a fifteen-minute lunch break when she would eat moldy bread and cheese and drink stale water, and then right back to work. Frankie got plenty to eat working for the street vendor — until he realized the vendor was subtracting the cost from his weekly pay, which wasn't much to begin with.

"I finally found us a room once Frankie stopped eating so much and we scraped together the money," Sally continued. "It was a six-story walk-up and wasn't much better than the flop, since the family we rented from wanted us out first thing in the morning and not back until even later at night. So after work I'd find Frankie and we'd walk the streets and find something to eat until it was late enough that they'd let us in our room. But at least when we were in our little room there wasn't anybody saying the kinds of ugly things we heard all the time at the flop or on the street. The only good thing was there were lots of street musicians out all the time, especially outside the bars, singing for their supper."

"You mean buskers!" I said. "Greg and I have done that before."

Sally looked at me for a minute, confused. "You lost your mama and papa, too? That how you made your way?"

"Oh no," I said. "Sorry. No. My parents are alive, and we didn't *have* to be buskers. We just liked doing it, and liked making money. That's all I meant."

Sally nodded. "Wish I'd played an instrument. I'd have done that, too, rather than what I was doing. That factory was the hottest place I've ever been, but if you sweated on anything you were sewing, they'd take it out of your pay the same as that vendor took it out of Frankie's for eating up the profits."

"What were you sewing?" I asked.

Sally laughed. "That's the funny thing. We were making uniforms for the army. Well, not the whole uniform, but the trousers and coats. It was machine sewing we were doing."

"You must have been exhausted by the end of the day each day," I said. "Frankie, too."

She nodded. "Bone tired. But it was what we had to do. And would have probably kept doing it, too, but then one day Frankie decided to go for a soldier without even telling me. They were putting together an Irish brigade, under Brigadier General Thomas Meagher, recruiters beating the bushes all over the city for red-blooded Irishmen, and offering a signing bonus. And thirteen dollars a month pay, room and board included!"

"So that was a lot back then?" I asked.

"Oh, you bet," Sally said. "Only they didn't take girls, and there Frankie was all of fifteen by then, and me just sixteen. He told me he did it so I wouldn't have to work those long hours anymore, and he said I had taken such good care of him that it was his turn to take care of me. But I knew that Frankie, as good-hearted a kid as he was, needed somebody to keep an eye out for him. And since there was no getting out of him signing on already, and since I'd promised Mama and Papa that I'd take care of him, I went down to where they were recruiting for their Irish brigade and I signed on, too. So we both got the signing bonus. That was about the only good thing. Me and Frankie, for the first time in our lives, and probably the last, we were rich! Even took ourselves out for a steak dinner! That was July of 1861."

"But how did you do it?" I asked. "You said yourself they wouldn't take girls."

"It was right easy," Sally said. "First thing was cut my hair to look like a boy's. Frankie actually did that for me. Got hold of some loose clothes, bound up my chest, dirtied my face some, put on a hat, tried to talk in a deep voice, or deep as I could. But heck, my voice was already deeper than Frankie's, and once my hair was short I already looked more like a boy than him and a lot of those other young fellows signing up."

"And they didn't do, like, some sort of physical exam?"

"Of course they did," Sally said. "Checked my teeth to make sure they weren't rotten and that I still had most of them — which I did and still do."

She showed me, just in case I doubted her.

"They made me march back and forth across the room to make sure I wasn't bowlegged," she continued. "Asked me if I had worms. Made me show them my fingers, too, to make sure I had them all, and especially the trigger finger, which is the most important. I told them I'd been shooting a gun since I was knee high to a grasshopper, and I even offered to show them if anybody had a musket. They said that wasn't necessary. Said they'd teach me everything I needed to know, and that was that."

"Why did they call it an Irish brigade?" I asked. "Because most of the people in it were Irish?"

Sally laughed. "Can't nobody call you a dummy," she said. "Some of those other units didn't want us Irish joining them. There was a lot of prejudice against the Irish, you know. All those hoity-toity New Yorkers afraid we'd come in and take the jobs that they thought belonged to them. Saying we were all nothing but a bunch of drunks and Catholics. Truth was, when Frankie and me were growing up, we hardly even knew we were Irish. Just knew we talked a little different from most in Schenectady. But there were guys in the brigade so Irish they still spoke the language, and hardly any English. And when they did speak English they mangled it so bad that Lord knows what they were saying. We turned out to be a tough bunch of fighters, though. And if you don't believe me just ask any of those Johnny Rebs we lit into at Antietam."

I'd heard of Antietam — I knew it was a battle in the Civil War — but that was about all. Sally must have seen it on my face because she filled me in. "Antietam, up there in Maryland. Bloodiest battle of the war. We fought the Rebels to a standstill, which wasn't much to brag about, but at least for once we didn't lose ground or lose as many men as them. The Irish Brigade was in the thick of it. Only I made sure they let Frankie stay behind the lines, running messages between the officers and such."

She got quiet for a minute. "It was the first time I took and fired my gun at anything real, besides deer and bird and squirrel," she said. "And close-up, too. So close you could see their faces, and them screaming and bawling like little kids once they were shot, or got the bayonet. Our boys did the same. Some right next to me. And there was nothing you could do about it. No way to save the ones that needed saving. No way to save yourself except keep fighting harder than anybody else, and keep being luckier than anybody else.

"So that's what I did. And dear Lord help me, but I was good at it, too."

CHAPTER 16

I had remembered to text Mom and Dad earlier, before talking to Sally, so they weren't mad at me when I came in late for dinner. Mom was still pretty tired from her fall and everything, and they spent the evening on the sofa in the living room watching TV while I retreated to my bedroom to fill Julie and Greg in on what I'd learned.

Greg was blown away.

"Wow," he said when I called. "I was just sort of going along with Julie when she said it was possible the ghost was a girl. I can't believe you got her name, too."

"Little Belman might have actually helped with that," I admitted.

"What? Did she come back or something?" Greg asked, confused.

"No. But I think all her yelling at the ghost about knowing the ghost was a girl helped trigger something. At least that's what it seemed like."

"Huh. Guess that kind of makes sense. But what about the last name?"

I was stumped. In my excitement to hear Sally's story, I'd totally forgotten to ask what her last name was.

"Well, at least we know what unit she was in," I said. "The Irish Brigade. I was going to research that tonight. I guess we need to find out as much as we can even faster now, since it's just a couple of days until December 11."

"The day the Union finally crossed the river," Greg said, practically finishing my sentence for me.

"Yeah," I said. "That was when they finally got the pontoons to the river, but that's about all I know so far."

"Have you talked to Julie yet?" Greg asked. "I bet she already knows everything about it. She's so smart. I wish I was half as smart as her."

"You are," I said, though I had my doubts about either one of us being even half as smart as Julie.

Greg just laughed, as if what I'd said was meant to be funny.

"You should go ahead and call her," he said. "I bet she'll totally grill you about the conversation with the ghost. Sam. Or Sally. Or whatever."

And she did. I called as soon as Greg and I hung up, and spent the next half hour getting the first degree from Julie: Why hadn't I found out the ghost's last name? What was Sally's commanding officer's name? What did Sally think happened to her little brother now that she was starting to remember so much stuff about their childhood, and how they ended up together in the Union army? Why did she choose the name "Sammy"? Was it just because of the alliteration — Sally and Sam — or was it something else? Did anyone in the Irish Brigade ever find out she was a girl? Was anyone suspicious?

Of course I didn't have answers to hardly any of Julie's questions, and it totally wore me out trying to keep up with the barrage of them, and trying to explain why I hadn't found out any of that stuff, and the whole time just wanting to crawl into bed and go to sleep. It hadn't just been a really long day. It had been a really, really long week. And I knew there was a lot more to come.

Finally, I heard Julie's mom ordering her to get off the phone, so she said good-bye and she would have more questions tomorrow, which was Saturday. She might text me some more tonight.

I groaned — and turned my phone off.

I knew I should get on the computer and read up more on the Battle of Fredericksburg, and Antietam, and the Irish Brigade and the river crossing. But it was getting late, plus I kept thinking about Sally and Frankie and how they lost both of their parents to tuberculosis and had to fend for themselves. I thought about how people were prejudiced back then against the Irish immigrants, which still didn't make any sense to me, but I guess there are always going to be people who think less of anybody who seems different from them. That's one of the things we kept seeing in our research into the different wars, to help out our different ghosts, and it was pretty depressing.

But still not as depressing as losing your parents.

I went into the living room and joined my mom and dad on the couch. Mom had fallen asleep and was leaning on Dad. I sat next to her on the other side and wished I could curl up in her lap the way I used to when I was little.

"Hey, buddy," Dad whispered. "Everything okay with you?"

I nodded. "Is Mom all right?" I asked.

"Oh, sure," he said. "Just tired. Couple of days in the hospital are enough to wear anybody out. We probably should see about helping her to bed."

We didn't do that right away, though. Maybe Dad just somehow knew that I wanted to be close to both of them at least for a few minutes. We sat there together and it felt nice. I don't even remember what dumb show was on TV. All I really heard was Mom's breathing, and Dad turning the pages on a magazine he was sort of reading and sort of not.

Finally, Mom opened her eyes halfway and struggled to sit up. She put her arm around me. "What a sweet little family we are," she said. "We sure have been together a lot lately, haven't we?"

I said we sure had, and Dad said he wouldn't have it any other way.

·   ·   ·

Saturday was super busy for everybody — it was chore day at my house, and I had to actually scrub the kitchen floor, if you can believe that. And vacuum every room! Greg and his dad liked to do special stuff on Saturdays, like go for hikes in the mountains, but since it was raining they went to not one but two movies. Ever since his dad stopped drinking, and Greg started going to Al-Anon meetings, he and his dad had gotten a lot closer, and Greg didn't come over nearly as often as he used to to spend the night with me.

Julie had a tae kwon do tournament on Saturday that she said would take up the whole day. She was on the tournament team, and did sparring and something called "forms," whatever that was. Until she told us, I hadn't even known she did tae kwon do.

Sunday afternoon we all were supposed to meet up at the Kitchen Sink for band practice, and I got there before the others. Well, almost there. I was a block away, just turning the corner onto Caroline Street on my bike, when somebody grabbed the handlebars and stopped me. It was Belman.

"Stay away from my little sister, dork," he ordered.

"What do you mean?" I asked, nervous, getting off my bike. I didn't know if he'd been waiting on me, or if he just happened to be there — but I didn't ask.

"My mom told me all about you Dopes of War scaring her, pretending one of you was a ghost," he said. "Deedee told me it was a real ghost, but then she changed her story. Now she won't talk about it, but I know she came back over here yesterday. You probably invited her. She won't talk about that, either. What are you doing, trying to get her to join your little band? Or do you have a crush on her? Is that it? You have a crush on my sister?"

I nearly fell over. "I don't have a crush on your sister," I said. "I don't even like her!"

That did not make him happy. "And just what's that supposed to mean?" he snarled.

I tried to recover. "I'm sure she's really nice and everything," I said. "I just meant, you know, I don't *like* like her. That's all. Plus, she's just in fifth grade."

"And you're a sixth-grade dork," he said. "So just stay away from her."

I couldn't believe this conversation. For one thing, I'd never had a girlfriend — I'd never even held hands with a girl. And Little Belman . . . definitely no way!

"Whatever," I said. "I mean, okay. I mean, I promise I'll keep not liking her. I mean, I'll keep not *like* liking her. And I won't talk to her. And I won't invite her over here, even though I didn't in the first place."

"You better," he said, standing so close over me that I got a kink in my neck looking up at him.

He deliberately bumped into my shoulder as he walked past, knocking me off balance as my bike crashed to the sidewalk. I might have fallen down if Greg hadn't shown up just then and caught me.

"What was that all about?" he asked. "You want me to go jump on him?"

"NO!" I practically shouted. "What the heck would you do that for?"

"It looked like he was threatening you," Greg said.

"Well, he sort of was," I said. "He didn't say what he was going to do to me, though. Anyway, he thinks I have a crush on his sister. He was telling me to stay away from her."

Greg went from angry to laughing his head off in the space of about a second.

"It's not that funny," I said, but he couldn't stop laughing. Julie came up just then and asked what was going on, and when Greg told her she cracked up, too.

This was turning out to be the weirdest week of my life.

CHAPTER 17

We hadn't seen the ghost — or one another — all day Saturday, and I was starting to wonder if we'd see her on Sunday. Julie's theory was that Sally had exhausted herself the day before dealing with Little Belman, telling me the secret about her identity that she'd kept from everybody except her brother for more than one hundred and fifty years, and remembering all about her parents and her childhood and joining the army and the Battle of Antietam.

"She probably doesn't have enough psychic energy to show up right now," Julie said. "I think when the ghosts stay away it can be because they need to recharge their batteries, so to speak."

"Or that their batteries are just running out and maybe can't be recharged," Greg added. "So to speak."

"Right," said Julie, who clearly liked it when Greg repeated the way she said things. I rolled my eyes. I didn't think much of their theories, but I didn't have anything better to suggest so just kept quiet.

We practiced for a while — all our old standards, plus without our even discussing it we launched into a rock-and-roll version of "The Battle Hymn of the Republic." I remembered Sally singing it with me — and then soloing — the day before, and wished she was there to sing it with us just then. That would have been cool.

After the last "Glory, glory, hallelujah," Julie decided we'd practiced enough. She also decided to fill us in on details about the Battle of Fredericksburg that she'd stayed up late the past couple of nights reading about.

"So tomorrow, December 11, is the big day," she said. "That was the day the Union army engineers finally got the pontoons down to the river, and the army started crossing over into Fredericksburg, but it got very complicated very fast."

"Like how?" Greg asked.

"For one thing it was just twenty-four degrees out, and they started at three in the morning, so it was freezing and it was hard to see. But at least the river wasn't frozen solid. The engineers had to anchor dozens of the pontoon boats side to side all the way across the river, which is pretty wide where they were trying to cross, and then build the bridges with planks on top of the pontoons."

"Wait," I said. "You said 'bridges' plural?"

"Right," said Julie. "Three pairs of bridges. One to cross at the north end of Fredericksburg, one to cross a mile away at the south end of town, and a third one downriver another mile farther beyond the town. Half of the Union troops, about sixty-five thousand men, would go across the first two bridges into town — they called those the Upper and Middle Crossings — and attack the main Confederate force at the Rebels' defensive position outside of town in Marye's Heights. Sally and her brother, Frankie, and the Irish Brigade would have crossed over there and been in that part of the battle.

"The other half of the Union force would cross farther downriver at what they called the Lower Crossing and hopefully surprise the Confederates by sweeping around behind them from the south and east. Only that's not what ended up happening."

"Why didn't it?" Greg asked.

"It was about as ridiculous as them having to wait so long to get the pontoons," Julie said. "Major General William B. Franklin was in charge of the troops at the Lower Crossing and he messed up his orders from General Burnside. On December 13, Franklin sent only thirty-eight hundred men to attack the Rebel line instead of all sixty-five thousand!"

Greg and I stared at Julie, bewildered.

"Why didn't he double-check with General Burnside?" Greg asked. "I mean, why would they send that many soldiers down there, but only want him to use a handful?"

"Yeah," I said. "That doesn't make sense at all."

Julie nodded. "I know. I told you it was ridiculous. But all the historians agree that the order General Burnside wrote down at about three o'clock in the morning, just hours before the attack, wasn't clear. General Franklin thought General Burnside wanted him to hold most of his troops back near the river. Just in case of, well, who knows? Nobody to this day has been able to exactly figure out why Franklin didn't send a messenger back to Burnside to double-check the order. The whole battle would probably have turned out totally different. So instead of the Union army overwhelming the Confederate defenses, the Confederates were able to push that one lonely Union division of General Franklin's back to the river without too much trouble. It was at this place we now know as Slaughter Pen Farm."

"I know where that is," I said. "We've driven past it a million times. It's a few miles from here."

"Right," said Julie. "Well, it turned out there were nearly forty thousand Confederate troops positioned up on high ground overlooking Slaughter Pen Farm, way more than anybody on the Union side thought. Even at that, one Union division still managed to break through the Confederate line — briefly. But then when there were no reinforcements sent in, the Yankees were forced back by the Confederate counterattack. I think there were something like five thousand Union casualties in that part of the battle, including some other smaller fights, and cannon fire back and forth. And four thousand Confederate casualties."

I could picture now where all that fighting had been at Slaughter Pen Farm, but what I couldn't picture was nine thousand men there — dead or wounded or injured or captured or missing in action.

But at least it was all starting to make sense — the geography of it, anyway. I knew the Rebel defenses and artillery had been lined up for miles south of Slaughter Pen Farm on what is now called Lee Drive. People drive there all the time to check out the old cannons and Confederate trenches and Robert E. Lee's lookout post high on what they used to call Telegraph Hill. It's part of the national park, although most people just ride bikes and jog and rollerblade up and down Lee Drive, not really thinking about what an important Civil War site it is.

"I wonder when we'll see Sally again," I said. "It would be good to ask her what she knew about Slaughter Pen Farm and the fighting on Lee Drive."

"I bet she didn't know anything about it," Greg said. "Because she was in town the whole time, and there wasn't any TV or radio or anything to let people know about what else was going on even just a few miles away. I mean, according to Julie, General Franklin didn't even ask General Burnside a simple question, like, 'Are you out of your mind? You just want me to send in one division?' "

"I wish Sally was here so we could just ask her," I said again.

"What happens if she doesn't show up?" Greg asked quietly. "How will we ever help her find out what happened — how she ended up missing, and how she died? What if she used up all her, what did you call it, Julie? — her psychic energy — telling Anderson everything on Friday, and now she's just, well, done."

"I can't believe that," I responded. "She was so excited to be remembering everything, as hard as it was to talk about. I had the idea that she felt sort of free, getting to tell somebody that she was really a girl. She didn't seem all staticky and fading in and out like our other ghosts did when they were nearing the end of their time being able to see us and talk to us and everything."

"I just hope it's what I said before," Julie said.

"You mean recharging her batteries?" Greg asked.

Julie nodded. "I'm not sure how that happens, exactly, except maybe it's like us taking a nap."

"Or going to sleep at night," I added, "which all this week I bet is something none of us have done very much of."

Greg yawned, as if to prove my point. Julie and I couldn't help it: we yawned, too. Then we all laughed, not that it was all that funny.

We waited another five minutes, none of us saying anything, all of us hoping. But in the end there was no Sally. Not that day, anyway.

CHAPTER 18

"It's started."

I was dreaming that the ghost had come into my room, looking a lot more Sam than Sally. Standing at the end of my bed and saying that:

"It's started."

"What has?" I replied in my dream.

"The pontoons, down to the river," the ghost said.

I opened my eyes and realized it wasn't a dream after all. The ghost *was* in my bedroom, and she *was* speaking to me from the end of my bed.

"What time is it?" I asked. "And how did you get here? I

thought you couldn't leave the building, or downtown, or whatever."

"It's two a.m.," Sally said. She looked around my room and seemed surprised to find herself there. "And I don't know how I got here. Wherever this is."

I told her it was my bedroom.

"We're at my house," I added. "We live just a couple of blocks from Sunken Road. When you were here for the battle it was all just open fields, but now it's a neighborhood."

Sally nodded, then said again, "Well, I just needed to tell you that it's started. They're sliding pontoons down to the river from the Chatham Heights."

"Is it working?" I asked. "I mean, did it work?" I was confused because Sally was speaking in the present tense, as if everything was actually happening right now, when of course it all happened a hundred and fifty years ago.

"Nah," Sally said. "Too steep. Crashing down too fast." She switched to past tense. "So they switched up their tactics and had to haul those long pontoon wagons slow down the hill to the different crossing points."

"Then what?" I asked, sitting up in bed and checking my clock. Sure enough, it was now just a little after two. Another night I wasn't going to get much sleep.

"Putting the pontoons in the water, nailing on the planks, working fast as they could to get it done before the Rebels could figure out what was going on." Sally paused. "At least that's what I could see. We were at the Middle Crossing. So cold we were all shivering, waiting in our formations to make the crossing once those engineers were done. Only that didn't quite happen the way it was supposed to."

"So what happened?" I asked.

"Rebels woke up to what we were doing," she said. "They fired a couple of cannon shots, though they didn't hit anywhere near the pontoons. Then their snipers started shooting our engineers, so Old Burnside, he ordered our cannon to return the favor — all hundred and forty-seven of them. Figured if the Rebels were going to fire at us, we might as well unleash a barrage on the town where they were hiding. Especially since their sharpshooters started taking aim at the engineers. Our artillery boys sent a hundred shells a minute. You could see it as the sun rose — houses and buildings over there collapsing, chimney's toppling over, roofs catching fire. And our boys at the river's edge fired across with their muskets, too. But I guess they were shooting blind, 'cause the Rebels just kept on shooting at our engineers, finally chasing them off the bridge, which wasn't even half finished. I figured it must be the same on the other bridges, too, 'cause we could hear the rifle fire north of us, and the shouting." Her voice got lower, almost to a whisper. "And the screaming when one of them was hit."

Sally said the engineers waited until the shooting stopped on the Confederate side of the river, then they ventured back out onto the unfinished pontoon bridge and went back to work.

But as soon as they did, the Confederate sharpshooters started picking them off again. So again they retreated. Again the cannons roared until the sharpshooters' rifles quieted down. Once again, though, as soon as the engineers went back to work, the shooting commenced and more Union bodies fell into the river.

"I guess when the cannons were firing the Rebels must have retreated themselves to safer places," Sally said. "Or maybe they were just too well dug in and hidden. I'm sure some of them must have got hit by cannon, or trapped in those buildings that collapsed or caught fire or both. But not enough, 'cause that back-and-forth business went on into the afternoon. Only good thing for us — and for them — was it warmed up quite a lot. Frankie and me got sent on detail to help haul up the wounded to the hospital they set up at the Chatham Manor. Must have made a dozen trips back and forth. 'Course I made Frankie wait back at the tree line and not expose himself there too close to the river and those Rebel sharpshooters, even though they weren't taking so much aim at us as they were just the engineers."

"How did you ever get across, then?" I asked. Julie had told us there were complications, but I didn't know things had gotten *this* complicated.

"Somebody pointed out that pontoons were the same thing as boats, and why didn't we fill some of them up with our boys and their rifles and paddle across quick as they could and attack the Rebels over on their side, roust out all those snipers hidden up in there and clear out the town. Everybody knew General Lee's main army was well on the other side of town, hidden up on those hills where they'd have the advantage on us. They weren't all there in the town, 'cause they'd have been too close to our cannon."

"So that's what they did?" I asked.

"You bet they did," Sally said. "Wish they'd have sent my unit over, but they sent the 89th New York first. Half a dozen boats where we were. Probably forty men in each, some of them paddling with the butts of their rifles. Brave boys, let me tell you. Those Rebel sharpshooters kept firing but didn't nobody turn back, though I did see one of them pontoon boats paddling in a circle, not making much headway for quite a while. Finally, though, enough of them made it across, and then the fighting started right there in the streets. From what I heard, the fighting at the upper crossing was a whole lot worse. Somebody said they sent the 7th Michigan over at the Upper Crossing — even before the 89th New York went over down where we were at the Middle Crossing — then once those Michiganders got a toehold on the Fredericksburg side, they sent in the Harvard Regiment — bunch of Massachusetts boys. I heard later on that there was fierce fighting not just street to street but door to door, starting at the north end of town and working their way south to meet up with the Middle Crossers in the center of town and drive out the Rebels. Took quite a while, though, and quite a lot of casualties, 'cause the Rebels were shooting down on our soldiers from upstairs windows, rooftops, hiding behind walls, you name it. A third of the Harvard Regiment went down as casualties. But God bless 'em, our engineers were finally able to get back to their work and they finished up those pontoon bridges in just about no time. Once that happened, you bet General Burnside sent plenty of the rest of us pouring across to join the fight."

Sally smiled, but it wasn't a happy smile. More like a satisfied smile, I guess you could say. But like every ghost soldier we'd met, there was sadness there, too.

"All those Confederates holed up in Fredericksburg, they either died there that day, or they finally turned and ran back to join old General Lee outside of town up there on Marye's Heights where they had their fortifications. They left the town to us — or what was left of it, anyway."

CHAPTER 19

I don't know how long we talked — or, rather, how long Sally talked and I listened, asking the occasional question, until my yawns started to run together, despite how totally fascinating her story was. But I couldn't help myself. I got so tired that everything looked bleary to me, so much so that I couldn't even read the clock on my bedside table.

"I've kept you too long," Sally said when she finally noticed how I was drooping. "Sorry about that. It's just, I guess you do remind me of Frankie in some ways, and Frankie and me used to talk and talk and talk, sometimes practically all night. And by that I mean Frankie let me run my mouth about anything and everything. I know I probably took too much advantage of that. But spending so much of my day pretending to be somebody else other than who I really was, it was awful nice to get to just talk to somebody who knew me — the real me — and that I was a girl. *Am* a girl."

Sally paused for a second, then stood as tall as she could, like she was at attention. "One more thing I remembered," she said. "Almost forgot it again."

Then she saluted. "Private Sam Keegan," she announced. "Army of the Potomac. Second Army Corps. First Division. Second Brigade. 88th New York Regiment, Company G."

I grabbed a piece of paper and wrote it all down quickly, before I could forget.

We both smiled. Hers faded first. "And don't forget about Frankie," she said, her voice already sounding far away.

I'd pointed out to Greg and Julie that Sally didn't do any of that flickering business that we'd seen in our other ghosts as time seemed to be running out on us solving their mystery. But now, there in my room, Sally was doing just that — flickering, getting staticky, fading in and out. I suddenly had a million more questions for her, but it was too late.

Sally flickered one last time and then disappeared. I was so dopey and tired that I actually reached out for her, as if I could take hold of her arm and keep her there, which was absurd. I even said out loud, "Wait, Sam. I mean *Sally*!" But that's just how tired I was. I went to sleep soon after.

. . .

We had no school on Monday for one of those professional development days for teachers, so Julie, Greg, and I met up early at the Kitchen Sink, where I filled them in on everything Sally had told me in the middle of the night. I could tell they were disappointed that Sally had come to my house and not theirs — though that's how it had been with all our ghosts so far: They showed up at the Kitchen Sink, at my house, and sometimes other places like school or the backseat of Uncle Dex's car, but only if I was there. I couldn't explain why it was that way, any more than I could explain why Julie and Greg could see and speak to the ghosts in the first place — and why I could — but nobody else.

Well, nobody else except Little Belman. That was another whole mystery that I just didn't have the brainpower to try to figure out just then.

Julie got over her disappointment quickly, and peppered me with a hundred questions about what Sally had told me the night before. "Now that we have a last name, and her regiment and company and everything, plus her brother's name, we should be able to find out a lot more," she said. "I'll look it up tonight."

Greg asked a few questions, too, but he really didn't need to bother. Julie had covered pretty much everything. And when she saw that I didn't have any more answers, she took over the story where Sally had left off with the river crossings and the street fighting and the occupation of Fredericksburg.

"I read that things got a little crazy after they chased off the Confederates," she said. "Or a *lot* crazy."

"How?" Greg asked. "What?"

"Yeah," I echoed. "How?"

Julie gave us her disapproving look. "So I'm guessing neither of you has done much research on your own?"

We didn't answer. I guess we didn't need to, though we'd both done *some*. Just, well, not as much as Julie.

Julie sighed. "Okay. Well, whatever. But we're all supposed to be working on this together, you know?"

"We have been," Greg said. "Just not all in the same way. Anyway, um, maybe you could tell us what you found out, and then give us some reading assignments."

"Fine," Julie said. "Your assignments are once we leave here we should ride our bikes over to some of the important sites of the battle."

"Why wait?" I asked. "Let's go now."

So we did. First we went from downtown over the Chatham Bridge out of Fredericksburg and over to the Stafford County side of the river. Once we were there, we rode our bikes up a steep hill to Chatham Manor, which was where everything started for General Burnside and the Union army. In front of the mansion, facing the river, were these incredibly gnarled-up trees — they were called catalpas. They definitely looked like they should have fallen over already and died, except they were being propped up by braces because they were such important and famous trees. We read about it on one of the plaques. This famous poet, Walt Whitman, helped take care of casualties after the battle and he wrote about surgeons in Chatham Manor having to amputate hands and feet and arms and legs and tossing them outside the window and all the amputated limbs piling up under the catalpa trees.

Greg and I shivered when we read that. Julie did, too, even though she usually wasn't too affected by things like that. We went farther out on the grounds in front of Chatham

Manor to the cannons that were still there, aimed from Chatham Heights across the river at Fredericksburg, which we could see as clearly as anything. They also had a replica of the pontoon wagons that the engineers had used for building the bridges. Sally wasn't kidding when she said they were huge and heavy. No wonder they'd been so hard to transport all the way here.

"So this is where they blasted away at Fredericksburg with all the Union cannons," I said.

"And where they brought the pontoons down to the river," Greg said.

"And it was one of their hospitals, of course," I added.

"And one of their headquarters," Greg also added. "There were a couple of different mansions like this that belonged to Confederate sympathizers or whatever that the Union generals took over. I did read something about that. I think it was on a brochure from the battlefield Visitor Center. Did I tell you guys I went there?"

"No," I said. "But it's not very far from your house."

"We've all been there," Julie reminded us. "On field trips in elementary school? Remember? Hello?"

Greg shrugged. "I might have been too busy running around to notice *where* we were," he said. "We probably could have gone to Mars on those field trips and I wouldn't have exactly noticed."

Julie sniffed. I could tell Greg didn't like that, but he didn't say anything.

"Sally was here," I said. "Or near here. And her brother. It's weird to think about. They were with their brigade, I guess, camped in fields over here for, like, three weeks. Waiting for those pontoons."

"And going on those scouting missions," Greg reminded me.

"And helping those escaped slaves to freedom," Julie said. "If you think about it, the Rappahannock River was one of the dividing lines between North and South during the Civil War, and a dividing line between slavery and freedom."

She sounded like a tour guide, but it was still cool thinking that our river, and our town, played such a giant role in the Civil War and in the history of America.

"Anyway, now we have our panoramic view," Julie said. She pointed to different places on the river. First to our right, near what was now the Falmouth Bridge. "Upper Crossing," she said. Then to our left and the Chatham bridge we'd just come over on our bikes. "Middle Crossing." And finally she gestured to the railroad bridge down near the city docks. "Another mile down that way was the Lower Crossing."

We stared at each spot until Julie drew our attention back to the town, and the line of hills just beyond. We could see some of the redbrick buildings of the college up on those hills. Just like nearly all of the houses there, the college — actually a university now — hadn't been in existence during the Civil War. It was where the Confederate troops dug in their defenses, and waited for the Union attack.

"So what about the crazy part you mentioned before?" Greg asked. "Is that something we're supposed to be able to see from here, too?"

"No," said Julie. "That all happened back in town, and not in any one place in particular, but really all over. The Union soldiers went on a rampage and started looting and partying all over what was left of Fredericksburg. Dragging couches and beds out into the streets, stealing whatever of value they could lay their hands on. Setting more fires to stuff. They even dragged pianos outside and played on them and sang and danced around fires they set in the middle of the streets. Some of the soldiers even put on dresses they confiscated from some of the houses. And they consumed all the food and alcohol they could find. There were a lot of letters written by soldiers that recounted everything. And diaries by the Fredericksburg people who, for some reason, had stayed in town and so witnessed it all."

"How long did it go on?" I asked. "Didn't they have a battle to fight?"

"I'm sure in some places it went on all night," Julie said. "General Burnside wanted to wait another day to keep planning his attack, which was probably not very smart since it just gave General Lee more time to build up his defenses and plan his strategy for repelling the Union army once they did attack. At some point they started arresting soldiers who were doing the looting and vandalism. Southerners all over the Confederate states were outraged when word got out about what the Union soldiers had done. Nobody had ever heard of soldiers looting a conquered city before, at least not in America. And definitely not by Americans."

CHAPTER 20

I'd always thought of the Union soldiers the same way I'd always thought about the Allied soldiers in World War II — that they were the good guys, fighting to right a terrible wrong. So I wanted to believe that they were always good in the ways they behaved during the wars, too. But it was pretty clear, now that we were helping our fourth ghost solve our fourth ghost mystery, that the good guys could sometimes be not so good, too, even if they were on the right side overall.

Greg was thinking something different. "I wonder if maybe they were just, you know, so angry and upset about the Confederate sharpshooters shooting the Union engineers, and the people who lived in Fredericksburg letting the Rebels use their houses and businesses to hide in while they were doing it," he said. "I bet I'd be pretty mad, too, if it was my friends or my fellow soldiers who were getting shot. Or if it was me getting shot at. And knowing that everybody in town not only helped the snipers, but hated me and my friends and what we were fighting for. I bet I'd not care too much about all their stuff, and I might take what I wanted, or even destroy some things, too."

"That wouldn't be the right way to be," Julie said. "But I also think I understand."

"Well, either way," I said, "it sounds like what happened with all that vandalism was nothing compared to what was about to happen in the actual battle. I'm not even sure why we're talking about it."

Greg and Julie acted surprised that I'd said that. At least I thought that's why they looked so surprised all of a sudden. But then I realized they were staring at something behind me, so I turned to look, too, thinking maybe Sally had made her way over to Chatham.

But she hadn't. It wasn't Sally. It was Little Belman.

She was hiding — though not very well — in a little gazebo, next to a statue of Pan, the Greek god who was half goat and half human, or at least half human form. It was weird to see him in the Chatham Manor garden, and even weirder with Little Belman peeking out from behind Pan's goat butt.

"What are you doing here?" Julie shouted. "Are you following us?"

But Little Belman didn't answer. She stepped out from behind Pan, hesitated for a second, and then ran away. Greg started to chase her, but Julie stopped him.

"Let her go," she said. "Let's just get on our bikes and ride out to Slaughter Pen Farm and see if she follows us there. It's a few miles out of town and I bet she doesn't."

"But why is she following us in the first place?" Greg asked.

"Who knows?" I said. "She's just weird. And she thinks she saw a ghost."

We got on our bikes and rode down a long, steep gravel driveway to River Road, which was paved and which followed the edge of the Rappahannock. It was just a little ways on River Road back to the Chatham Bridge and into town, and then on to Slaughter Pen Farm. I couldn't help but think about the Union engineers and soldiers and the wheels of the pontoon wagons creaking over some version of this same road a hundred and fifty years ago, at two in the morning, getting ready for the crossings.

We decided to stop downtown to get some lunch first, though, and went into Goolrick's Pharmacy to get grilled cheese sandwiches, pickles, and potato chips. We also split a chocolate milkshake. I wasn't sure where Little Belman went while we ate — maybe down to her house to get her own lunch.

She was back to following us once we finished and climbed back on our bikes, though. We had to be really careful riding out to Slaughter Pen Farm because there was no sidewalk for much of the way, and the road was pretty busy, but we kept to the shoulder the whole time, and I was relieved to look back and see that Little Belman did, too.

Slaughter Pen Farm was just that — a farm, a house, a barn, a couple of big shade trees, and a wide expanse of fields that were now another part of the National Park. It was just off the highway. We'd driven past it all our lives and never thought much about it, but now we knew it for what it was — a giant failure of communication that was the site of one of the biggest blunders of the Civil War. We didn't stay too long there because there wasn't much to see. Julie pointed to a small hill where a Confederate officer named Pelham with a single cannon kept half the Union army ducking for cover for nearly an hour. Then she pointed to the tree line at the far end of the fields where a Union general named Meade led the one charge that broke through the Confederate line, until the Rebels regrouped. She pointed to the line of retreat where Meade's division backed out of the fighting, and where the Confederates knew better than to give chase because almost sixty thousand more Union soldiers were down by the river.

Little Belman stayed on her bike near the road and took off once again as soon as we got back on our bikes and rode out of Slaughter Pen Farm. She must have hidden somewhere, because we next rode a couple of miles over to Lee Drive to see where the Confederate defenses had been — even though we'd also been there a million times before. But we were all seeing with very different eyes now, and everything seemed different. Lee Drive was no longer just this nice place to jog or ride bikes. It was where the Civil War could have been shortened by a couple of years if the Union had prevailed, and it was where thousands of Americans fighting Americans died in the attempt.

Near the south end of Lee Drive, close to a place called Hamilton's Crossing, was a twenty-five-foot-tall stone pyramid that had been raised there after the war. It was next to the train track so that when people rode by on the train to and from Richmond they would see it and remember that this was the place where half of the Battle of Fredericksburg was fought.

It was getting to be late afternoon, maybe an hour of sunlight left, and we had the whole length of Lee Drive to ride north to get to Lafayette Boulevard and then home, a good five miles in all, so we set off, all of us tired, but still having to pedal up and down a bunch of rolling hills. We hadn't seen Little Belman for quite a while so thought she must have long since gone home, but then Greg caught sight of her behind us.

"Oh man!" he said. "That kid is *still* there!"

We all stopped and turned to look. Little Belman stopped, too, maybe fifty yards behind us.

"Come on," said Greg. "Let's just go. She'll keep following us. There's one more stop we should make before we go home."

"Where?" I asked.

"The National Cemetery," he said. "Where they buried a lot of the Union soldiers."

The cemetery was along Sunken Road and we'd all been there before, of course, usually on Memorial Day when the Boy Scouts set up and lit thousands of luminarias — bags with candles in them — at the graves. The graves were spread out in tiers, rising up the side of a steep hill, with thousands more graves covering several acres at the top. There were also some statues up there, some cannons, some monuments, some big shade trees. Mostly it was just peaceful. Well, peaceful and sad.

We parked our bikes at the entrance and hiked up to the top and just sat there for a long time, not speaking, all seeing things differently, I suspected, than we'd ever seen them before. Looking down on Sunken Road, where the worst of the next day's battle took place, and knowing that thousands died there, made it even sadder.

The sun was going down when we descended back to our bikes. Little Belman was still there, too, half hiding behind a tree next to the Visitor Center. She looked scared.

Julie took control of the situation. "Oh, just come on and join us!" she called out to Little Belman. "It's getting late and you shouldn't be out here by yourself. Don't worry, we won't be mean to you."

"Yeah," I added. "We just want to make sure you get home safely."

Little Belman hesitated, then came over to where we were, pushing her bike.

"How about if we just ride with you to your house?" Julie asked.

Little Belman looked mad, but she also looked a little anxious.

"We won't even ask you again why you've been following us," I said. "Don't worry."

Little Belman nodded but didn't say anything. So we got back on our bikes and left, with her following a little ways behind. I thought she'd speak at some point on the way to her house, give us a clue about why she was there and had been there for the past couple of hours, but she didn't. It had something to do with her knowing about Sally — though she didn't exactly know about Sally, since I had chased her off from the Kitchen Sink the other day before Sally finally told me that she was a girl.

But Little Belman did know there was a ghost. And she had her strong suspicions about Sam being Sally.

She still didn't speak when we stopped at her house. She just rode her bike around to her backyard and that was that.

"What a weird kid," Greg said.

"Oh, I don't know," I said. "People probably say the same thing about us."

Julie sniffed. "Speak for yourself, Anderson." And then off we went, heading home.

CHAPTER 21

I fished around on the Internet
that night until I actually found a casualty list for Sally's
regiment in the Irish Brigade — the 88th New York Volunteers.
I couldn't believe it. I mean, what great luck.

My happiness didn't last too long, though, because scroll-
ing down the list it wasn't long before I found Sally, or rather
Sam Keegan. All it said was "Age, 16 years. Enlisted at New
York City, to serve three years, and mustered in as private,
Company G, on October 2, 1861. Promoted corporal, no
date. Wounded and missing in action; December 13, 1862,
at Fredericksburg, Va; no further record."

That stopped me cold. I read the notation a dozen times,

trying to get my head around it. It all seemed so final. And Sally's whole life, or her time in the army, anyway, summed up in just those three little lines.

But at least Frankie's name wasn't on the casualty list, and that was something good that I would get to tell Sally, and that I bet would make her happy.

My phone vibrated with a text. It was Julie, telling me she had just found out the same thing as I had. She was even on the same website, which made me feel pretty smart. Then Greg buzzed in. He had found it, too.

Nice! I texted back.

Sad about Sally, Greg texted. *And still the mystery.*

But good about Frankie, Julie texted, echoing what I'd been thinking. *Will help Sally to know.*

. . .

The next day was uneventful, except that all three of us got in trouble in our three different classes in the morning at school for dozing off.

"I'm just glad tomorrow is December 13," Julie said when we met up at lunch and shared our stories about sleeping in class. "At least I think I am — if Sally will remember all the rest of her story, and we can finally help her find her answers."

"I just can't wait to tell her about Frankie," I said.

"Yeah," said Greg. "Wish we knew what happened to him after the Battle of Fredericksburg — if he survived the rest of the war, if he got to live for a long time and make something good of his life."

I thought about that, and then, for no real reason, said, "I just have this feeling that he did."

Julie and Greg nodded slowly, as if they had that feeling, too, even though none of us could explain why.

.   .   .

We got together at the Kitchen Sink for band practice, but really in hopes that Sally would show up. We were all still so tired that practice was terrible anyway, so we ended early. There wasn't an All-Ages band competition in December, so I guess it didn't matter that we weren't practicing all that much. I promised I would call Julie and Greg if Sally showed up at my house again that night, and Greg said, "You better."

"We'll come right over," Julie added. "We'll want to see her, too. It shouldn't be just you, Anderson."

"You're going to sneak out of your house?" I asked, not believing she would.

"Well . . ." Julie thought about it. "Maybe if Greg came over and got me and we came over together."

"Sure," Greg said. "I could do that."

"Okay," I said, still not believing it would happen. I figured Greg would sneak out for sure, but not Julie. "Anyway, it's not like I can summon her to appear, or that I'm just waiting until you guys aren't around to see her, you know."

"We know," Greg said, though he sounded just a little suspicious.

They rode off together on their bikes, but I stayed back to sweep the floor, something I'd been doing lately as a way to repay Uncle Dex for letting us use the basement for our band practice. Julie, Greg, and I were planning to try busking again soon — street performing — to raise some money for Uncle Dex, too. The broom seemed to kick up more dust than it swept, so I dragged out what must have been an antique vacuum cleaner and plugged that in. It made an industrial-level roar as I went through the store, careful not to knock anything over as I got up what dirt and dust that I could. Really, the whole place needed a good wiping down, but I wasn't about to take on that project.

Uncle Dex was long gone, so I locked up with the store key he'd given me. But then I stopped short, because who should be sitting there on her bicycle on the sidewalk next to my bicycle but, once again, Little Belman.

"Oh geez," I said. "Don't you ever just be, you know, home?"

"It's a free country," she said. "I can be wherever I want."

"Okay, well whatever," I said, climbing on my bike. "I'm leaving, so I guess you can keep sitting right here the rest of the night."

"Wait," she said, suddenly not sounding so, well, so like herself.

I looked at her.

"Is she?" she asked.

"Is she what?" I asked back.

"The soldier. The ghost," she said. "She's a girl, isn't she?"

I hesitated, not wanting to say anything to confirm that there even was a ghost. The less Little Belman knew — or could be sure she knew — the better.

"I don't know what you're talking about," I said. "You really have a big imagination."

She narrowed her eyes to glare at me. But that didn't last.

"Nobody will believe me," she said. "Not my mom, not Morris, not anybody."

"Who's Morris?" I asked.

Little Belman sighed with exasperation. "Morris Belman? Hello? He's my brother? The one you and your friends dropped eggs and my rubber chicken on?"

I started laughing, though I knew I shouldn't. It would only make her mad. But I couldn't help it. "Oh," I finally said. "Him."

"I just need to know about the ghost," she said, changing the subject. "Is she a girl — which I know she is. And what happened to her? And what's going to happen to her? I want her to be all right."

It was practically a speech, coming from Little Belman. But I still wasn't going to confirm anything for her. I said, "Let's just say that if there was a ghost — and I'm not saying there is, because there's no such thing as ghosts — but if there was one, and if that ghost happened to have been a Union soldier in the Civil War, then, um, okay, so maybe the ghost could have been a girl dressed like a boy, and maybe some people might be helping the ghost find out the answers to the rest of your — or her — questions."

I realized in trying to dance around actually answering Little Belman I'd answered her anyway, and just about totally confirmed everything she suspected.

But she didn't ask anything else, which surprised me. I thought she'd be all over me with a bunch more questions, like a police detective, or like Julie. But she just took a deep breath in, let it out really slowly, and then said, "Okay. Well, just let me know what happens. I can see her so that means you have to include me, too."

And with that she climbed on her bike and pedaled away.

· · ·

I felt bad for Little Belman, who I was actually starting to think of not so much as "Little Belman" but as "Deedee." I don't know what I'd do if Julie and Greg didn't believe me about the ghosts I'd met — or rather if they weren't able to also see and talk to the ghosts, too. I'd probably lose my mind and go through life like a crazy person.

But since they were right there with me, it all seemed okay. Weird, of course. Very, very weird. But okay.

So I guess if I did sort of confirm the existence of Sally to Deedee, it might not be so bad.

As long as she wasn't up to something sneaky and devious, and totally trying to trick me. I mean, she *was* a Belman, after all.

I didn't have too long to mull all that over, though, because once again I'd managed to be late for dinner without calling or texting. Thankfully, Mom seemed to be all the way better from her fall, and she was in a pretty good mood. Dad still wasn't home because of the usual traffic jam on the interstate from DC, so we sat at the kitchen table and played Uno for half an hour. I won three games in a row, but Mom didn't seem to care. She smiled and called me a stinker.

CHAPTER 22

Sally showed up in my bedroom again early the next morning.

"Meet me at Federal Hill," she said. "As soon as you can."

It occurred to me that, except for Julie, I'd never had a
girl in my bedroom, even one pretending to be a boy, and
wearing a dirty, weathered blue Union army uniform.

"What time is it?" I asked, struggling to sit up in bed.

"Early o'clock," she said. Then she repeated what she'd
said before. "Meet me at Federal Hill. Tell the others."

"When?" I asked. "Right now? We have to go to school
today, remember? Isn't it, like, Wednesday?"

"It's December 13, 1862," Sally said.

She vanished before I could ask anything else. But I did anyway. "Sally! Did you just say it's 1862? Like, the *year* 1862! You know it's not really that, right? *Right?*"

She wasn't there to answer, though. And I hadn't had a chance to tell her the most important news — that Frankie survived the Battle of Fredericksburg.

. . .

Federal Hill is an enormous house at the top of the hill on Hanover Street at what used to be the southern edge of Fredericksburg. Union officers used it as their observation post because it overlooked the field of battle. They also had a hot air balloon for watching the battle and sending reports down from high above everything, but it kept getting blown off course and didn't work too well. A doctor's family owns Federal Hill now and restored it. They even put in a swimming pool where those Union officers once stood and watched the terrible scene below them. There were probably soldiers buried there under that pool. Every standing house after the bombardment got turned into a hospital after the battle, according to Julie.

"So where's Sally?" Greg asked that afternoon after school as we surveyed the neighborhood that had grown up over the past hundred and fifty years where there had once been just open fields, or mostly open fields, south of town.

I shrugged. "She just said to meet her here."

"The Irish Brigade would have marched down this hill," Julie said. "Or near here, anyway, over on George Street a block over, on their way into the battle. That's probably why she wanted us to come to this spot — to see what she saw."

While we waited for Sally, Julie told us some more about the day of the battle. "For one thing it was really foggy, so the Confederates who were positioned behind the stone wall at Marye's Heights didn't see the first Union soldiers attacking until they were about two hundred yards away and the fog lifted. Back then, everything in front of us, all the way to Sunken Road, was empty, except for some fences that cut through the field, and that the troops had to push through or climb over, which slowed them down. But that wasn't the worst of it."

"What was?" I asked

"That millrace, where Kenmore Avenue is now," Julie said, pointing down to the bottom of the hill. "Right down there. It was fifteen feet across and five feet deep, with three feet of water in it. Soldiers had to break ranks and tightrope walk over some narrow beams to get across, which slowed them down even more."

I was pretty sure we'd talked about that millrace before, but just to refresh my memory I asked Julie about it. Surprisingly, it was Greg who answered. "It was dug to bring water to run a couple of mills in town, or just south of town," he explained.

I turned to Julie. "You have taught him well," I said, trying to sound formal, or pretend-formal, anyway.

Greg grinned. Julie just looked annoyed.

There was still no Sally, but we did have a fourth person with us, as it turned out. And once again it was Deedee Belman. Greg was the first to spot her, peeking out from behind a parked car half a block away. "Oh, great," he said. "She's back."

I suggested we just invite her to join us. Greg and Julie asked me if I had lost my mind, so I quickly filled them in about my conversation with Deedee the evening before.

Then, without waiting for them to respond, I waved to Deedee. "Come on," I yelled. "You can hang out with us."

Deedee stood up, hesitated, then picked up her bike and slowly walked it toward us down the sidewalk next to Federal Hill. "The ghost told me to come here," she said.

"Really?" Julie said. "We're supposed to believe that?"

"It's true," Deedee said. "And anyway I have a right to be here, too, you know."

"Yeah, yeah," I said. "It's a free country. We get it. It's okay. I invited you to join us, so let's all just get along for a minute and see what happens."

"You mean wait for the ghost," Deedee corrected me.

None of us would confirm that, but if Sally had really shown up at Deedee's house the same way she'd shown up at mine this morning, then I guess we didn't have to. I could tell Greg and Julie weren't at all happy about this turn of events, though, so I took them aside and made the case for letting Deedee stay.

"Look, for some reason she can see Sally, and she was the first to figure out Sally was a girl, and Sally invited her here. That has to be true, because how else would she have known to come?"

We argued about it back and forth for a few minutes. I wasn't even totally sure why I was making the case for Deedee to be there with us, but Greg and Julie finally, reluctantly, agreed that she should stay. "But she better not mess anything up," Greg said.

"And this better not turn out to be a trick," said Julie, echoing what I'd wondered myself the night before.

"Well, the good news is nobody believes her, or at least that's what she told me," I said. "Also, I found out Belman's first name. It's Morris."

"I always thought he looked more like a Derek," Greg responded. I had no idea what a Derek would look like myself. Then again, I had no idea what a Morris would look like, either.

We didn't get a chance to discuss it any further, or to make fun of Belman's name, because Sally showed up. Suddenly. Standing right beside us. Deedee let out a little chirp of surprise but quickly settled down and acted like she was one of us, which I guess now she sort of was.

"The Irish were down by the city dock," Sally said, as if we'd already been in the middle of a conversation about the day of the Battle of Fredericksburg and she was picking up where she'd left off. "That's where we made camp after the crossing. Had to sleep in the mud, what sleep anybody got. Bugle sounded reveille, and breakfast wasn't much. Just coffee, pork, and hardtack, then they called us to ranks and we lined up. Word went around that General Burnside wasn't sending the whole army in at once. There wasn't room. We'd be going across that field in waves, a couple of brigades at a time. So there we were, guns loaded and powder dry. Must have been midday before the first wave went in. All we could do was stand and watch it happen."

I tried to imagine what it must have been like, how Sally's heart must have been pounding, and how scared she must have been, no matter how brave she also was. "Julie told us about the open fields, and the fences, and the millrace," I said.

"Yeah," Greg added. "And she said the bridges were torn up so you all had to break ranks and walk single file over the steel beams."

Sally nodded. "Did she tell you that it made easy targets for the Confederate sharpshooters to take aim at our boys as they crossed over like that? And did she tell you that cannon fire came at us from different directions, scattering units all out of formation and killing left and right?"

We were silent.

"Well, that's what happened," Sally said. "And that wasn't nearly the worst of it. The worst was the Johnny Rebs behind that stone wall must have had their orders to hold fire until our boys in that first wave were a hundred yards out. One of their officers held his hat up way high, and when he dropped it those Confederates behind the stone wall fired for ten minutes without stopping. The smoke got so thick we couldn't see anything about what was happening down on the field."

Sally paused. "And then they stopped. I guess to let the smoke rise up off the field so they could see. And so we could see, too. But it wasn't something anybody should have to ever look at. There were hundreds of our boys from the Third Division, under General William French, lying dead. Word filtered back up the ranks from men closer to the slaughter about what all else there was on that battlefield: boys shot in all parts, with their heads, hands, legs, arms shot off and mangled. Somebody said it looked like a giant hog pen and all of them killed. Nobody made it any closer than fifty yards to that wall."

Deedee, who'd been standing next to me, I guess because she thought I was her only friend, started shaking. I let her lean against me and that seemed to help some. I felt all shaky on the inside, too, but tried not to show it. Julie and Greg were both blinking, as if they were trying to hold back tears, or just were having a hard time imagining what Sally was describing.

For a minute it seemed as if all the houses between Federal Hill and that murderous stone wall disappeared, and the actual battlefield in front of us was back the way it had been on that awful, awful day. Judging from the look in Sally's eyes, that's what she was seeing, too.

"They ordered in the next wave, and the next one after that," she said, "and it was the same as the first. We'd seen that level of slaughter before, of course — at Antietam. They had a sunken road there and when we overran it those poor Rebels trapped there suffered the same fate as our boys were suffering now. But the difference was it didn't stop this time. The difference was they ordered in that next wave.

"And then they ordered in us."

CHAPTER 23

Sally started walking slowly down the hill in the direction of Sunken Road. Several cars had passed by while we were standing next to Federal Hill, but if anybody saw anything unusual, they didn't show it. I figured it just looked like four kids standing around, talking, leaning on their bikes, hanging out after school.

We followed along next to Sally, walking our bikes, retracing the steps of the Irish Brigade where Hanover Street merged with George Street halfway down the hill. "I told Frankie to stay behind me no matter what," Sally said. "He was so scared, he could hardly breathe. I even told him that, too: to keep breathing. And to keep behind. I told him if anything happened to me, if I got shot, to keep behind me then, too. To lie right down on the ground behind me. No bullet would reach him that didn't go through me first. I told him I would protect him. And you know what he said to me? He said, 'None of this is right, Sissy.' He told me he ought to be helping the wounded off the battlefield and taking care of them back at the field hospital, not marching down this road, getting ready to kill the Confederates."

"Wait," said Julie. "There's something we didn't tell you yet, Sally."

I had wanted to be the one to give Sally the good news about Frankie, but I guessed it was okay that Julie did it, since she'd found out about it, too.

"He lived!" Julie said. "We found the casualty list and he wasn't on it. That means he survived the battle!"

Sally froze at the news. I believe she would have cried, except she'd spent so much time pretending to be a guy — and not just a guy but a tough soldier of a guy — that she probably didn't know how anymore, or couldn't afford to, in case someone might suspect who she really was. Not that boys can't cry, too, of course. It's just that a lot of people — and especially back then — don't think they should.

"That's a heavy burden off my shoulders and my heart," she whispered, her voice cracking. "Thank you, thank you, thank you."

"You're welcome," Julie said. "I just wish we were able to find out more about Frankie for you, but it was so long ago."

"That's plenty right there," Sally said. "Plenty enough to know he lived another day. And I can have my hopes that he got to do just what he said — go back to one of those field hospitals and help those who were suffering, instead of being the one to inflict the suffering. It wasn't in his nature to ever hurt nobody."

We all stood there for a few minutes longer until Sally seemed ready to push on. There was a battle still raging all around us — or at least there had been a hundred and fifty years before — and we had to go deeper into it to find out what happened to our ghost.

Sally confirmed it. "Now if I can just find out how I came to be missing," she said. "That might be the last thing I need to know."

· · · ·

Sally continued talking as we walked. "General Meagher — he was the one that formed the Irish Brigade and the one that gave us our battle order — told us to all pull a sprig of leaves off some boxwood bushes, and tuck it into our hats. He said it was green for Ireland. We all did what he said, and we all listened to what else he said, too, 'cause he could see what we'd seen, and he knew what was coming up on us once we charged across that field."

She swallowed, then continued. "He said, 'This may be my last speech to you, but I will be with you when the battle is the fiercest; and, if I fall, I can say I did my duty, and fell fighting in the most glorious of causes.' I'll always remember that."

She kept walking and talking. "There were four brigades that had already attacked Sunken Road and the stone wall and Marye's Heights, and we were determined that they wouldn't need any more after the Irish Brigade was done taking the fight to those Rebels. We fixed bayonets when they ordered and kept marching right up from town. That Confederate artillery opened up as soon as we got in their range. Shells exploding overhead, shot bouncing off of what buildings there were, tearing through the ranks. One shell hit the 88th New York and we must have lost two dozen men all at once."

Sally shook her head. "We didn't turn back, though. We couldn't. We broke into a jog and kept right on at them —

me once again making sure Frankie stayed behind, as close to safe as possible, which, now you tell me, turned out to be safe enough, so hallelujah for that. We got to the bottom of this hill and climbed over or splashed through that millrace, then the officers called us to ranks again. General Meagher gave us the order to advance forward, double-quick, which of course we did, and next thing we knew we were out on that open plain, charging forward as hard and fast as we could go. Another thing slowed us down, though — the most terrible thing of all."

"More cannonballs?" Greg asked.

"Worse," Sally said. "Our own men. The ones on the ground, the ones that were wounded from the earlier waves, they grabbed at our trousers to try to stop us. 'Don't go,' they cried out. 'It's murder! It's murder!' But we couldn't stop. We pulled away. We ran around them. There were so many; I hate to say it but we even had to run over some of them, living and dead. All that running — all that hard charging — it only got us to that Rebel volley sooner, the closer we made it to their stone wall, and just like those brigades before us, the Confederates cut us down like hogs in a hog pen, too.

"A bullet tore through my cap," she continued, caught up in her own story. "I felt it whistle by my ear. Then I felt one slam into my arm and I went down but just for a second, then pushed myself back up with my rifle, only the bad thing happened then — the worst thing of all — which was I lost sight of Frankie. I called for him and called for him, but there wasn't time to go looking. We made it fifty yards from the Rebels and that's where we took our stand — firing back at them as fast as we could load and aim, which wasn't fast enough to keep even more of us from getting cut down. We didn't last but a couple of minutes and then our proud Irish Brigade dissolved just like the brigades that had come before us and just like the others that General Burnside would send in behind us. Some managed to turn and run back to town, back to safety. Some managed to crawl off the battlefield. I felt something explode into my side and down I went a second time only I couldn't get back up no matter how hard I tried, except to push myself behind a dead horse that had managed to get itself killed out there, but at least it was some protection, even if not much. Even if not much at all."

By this time we were at the National Park, a thin stretch of land at the old Sunken Road where they'd rebuilt the Confederates' stone wall, and restored one of the small wooden houses where Union soldiers had tried to hide from the Rebels' withering gunfire. Beyond, on the other side of the stone wall, was Brompton, which had served as one of the Confederates' headquarters, and which was now the university president's house. Next to that, with those tiers of grave sites going up the side of the steep hill, was the National Cemetery.

Sally had quit speaking. I imagined her, disguised as a young soldier, a boy, lying somewhere near where we stood, wounded, not able to move, with a dead horse the only thing keeping her from being hit and killed by more Confederate bullets.

"Why did they keep sending in more troops?" Greg asked. "I mean, you all didn't stand a chance. What was General Burnside even thinking?"

Sally shrugged. She seemed to be too deep in her own thoughts to care too much.

Julie answered. "He thought General Franklin was attacking the Confederate line to the south, from Slaughter Pen Farm. He didn't know that Franklin hadn't understood the orders and had sent only those 3,800 men. General Burnside was convinced that he had to keep Lee's troops occupied here at Sunken Road, so Lee couldn't send reinforcements to fight Franklin's troops. It was all a big, confusing, tragic mess. Plus, if General Burnside didn't send more men into the battle here, he wouldn't be able to offer any protection to all the men who were wounded and trapped on the battlefield. The Confederates would be able to just sit there and pick them off one by one. Which is sort of what happened anyway."

Sally came out of her reverie and nodded. "Between attacks, anybody that moved, they shot them. Wouldn't let hospital wagons out on the battlefield to take back the wounded or the dead. They all just had to lie there, same as me. Some couldn't move even if they wanted to. Some couldn't wait any longer for help and tried to crawl off the battlefield. Some made it. Most didn't."

There were seven waves in all. Julie knew the numbers. A third of the Irish Brigade went down as casualties. There were even more casualties from the other assaults. Nearly thirteen thousand Union casualties in all. The Confederates suffered a thousand wounded or killed. As terrible afternoon turned slowly into night, General Burnside was finally convinced not to send any more Union troops into the slaughter. What was supposed to have been an easy, surprise river crossing that could have led to an unobstructed march to Richmond and an early end to the Civil War had turned into the bloodiest battle and most lopsided Union defeat so far. There would be over two more years of awful, awful fighting before it was all over.

But Sally didn't know any of that at the time.

All she knew, lying there for hours and hours on the battlefield with thousands of others, bleeding, dying, not able to escape, was that the most curious thing started happening in the night sky. "I didn't know what it was at first," she told us. "I thought maybe I had already died and what I was seeing was heaven itself. But then I realized it was the northern lights, which I knew nobody ever saw this far to the south. And yet there it was, lighting up the sky with every color there is. I had never seen anything so beautiful. I didn't know what it meant, and I didn't have anybody to ask. I so desperately wished Frankie was there with me right then so we could see it together, and so I could know he was safe."

She paused again. "It was then, seeing the northern lights, that I resolved to not let myself die, to crawl wherever I had to go, to search the entire field, no matter how badly shot up I was, to find my little brother."

CHAPTER 24

Deedee had been so quiet since joining us that I'd forgotten she was even there. So it surprised me — surprised all of us — when she spoke.

"You loved your brother that much," she said quietly.

"I promised my parents," Sally said. "I had to find him."

"But what could you do?" I asked. "The Confederates would shoot at anything, or anybody, who moved."

"I moved anyway," Sally said. "Pushing myself into the mud, crawling on my belly with one arm, holding my wounded side with the other. I whispered Frankie's name. Men begged me to help them. They begged for water. Some had been lying in the field, wounded or just trapped, for hours and hours. I gave as much of my water as I could spare, but I had to save some in my canteen for Frankie. It was horrible. I couldn't tell what was mud I was crawling through and what was blood. The bodies seemed to spread out endlessly. Once, twice, I made too much noise and they shot at me. One shot hit my boot and tore off part of my foot. I was sure of it, but I couldn't afford to reach down to find out. The pain kept me conscious. I couldn't pass out. I had to find Frankie.

"But I never did."

I looked at the others when Sally paused there in her story. Everybody was crying, even Julie who never cried. Even Deedee. I put my arm around Deedee's shoulders and patted her, hoping that would help. I wished I could do something for Sally, but as close as she was to us, she was too far away for me to ever put my arm around her, too.

Without my fully realizing it, we had started walking away from Sunken Road, back toward town. We were on Mercer Street, one of the closest to the battlefield, and Sally stopped there, next to a brick house that looked like it dated back to the Civil War. There was a sign on it: THE STRATTON HOUSE.

"I remember this place," said Sally. "After hours in the battlefield, I had to give up on my search for Frankie. I hoped maybe he'd been able to escape the slaughter and I would find him in town. Maybe he was wounded and I'd find him at one of the houses that they'd turned into a hospital. Maybe he'd done what he said and was in one of those hospitals helping the surgeons, trying to save other soldiers."

"What about this place?" Greg asked.

"I made it this far, using a rifle for a crutch now, to hold myself up. But I staggered anyway, like a drunk man. There were men packed here inside and out, some living, more of them dead. The dead they rolled outside. The dead horses they used for breastworks, piling the bodies up high enough to act as a wall. I studied all the faces of the dead, but none of them was Frankie. So I staggered on toward town. I knew if I didn't get help for myself soon that I wouldn't last. But if I stayed there, or stopped moving anywhere along the way, I was dead, too. I had to find a hospital."

"But they would find out you were a girl," Deedee blurted out, only the second time she'd spoken since joining us what seemed like a hundred hours before, though really it was just then pushing five o'clock.

Sally nodded. "I thought of that. I was delirious, I guess you could say, but I still managed to think of it, and to think of what it would mean. They wouldn't let me stay in the army, and how would I ever take care of Frankie then? If I tried to reenlist in the same regiment, they'd know who I was and they wouldn't let me in. If I enlisted in another regiment, I wouldn't be with Frankie."

We kept walking back to town. I imagined wounded and dying men littering the ground all around us, which must have been the case. And I remembered reading that a lot of bodies of Union soldiers were buried right where they died, in people's yards, just about everywhere. I wondered if they could still be under us — and if Sally might be one of them.

But she said no. "Every time an ambulance wagon passed me I waved them away," she said. "I told them I was fine. Just bone weary from the battle. They had men stacked like cordwood — the living and the dead — and didn't have room for me anyway. They were glad to push on wherever they were going. I pushed on, too, the questions vexing me more and more, the closer I got to town: How could I pass for a soldier any more if I went to a hospital and put myself in the hands of the surgeons? The blood was running through my hands from the bullet hole in my side. I could hardly stand by the time I stumbled downtown. I needed time to think. I needed to lie down somewhere and rest, and think things through."

We were all the way back downtown now, on Caroline Street, actually standing in front of the Dog and Suds building, next door to the Kitchen Sink.

"It didn't look like this back then," Sally said. "Our cannon had taken off the roof, and the top floors. There was only the first floor left, and not much of that. Door hanging off the hinges. Windows blown out. Everything inside thrown upside down, or stolen, or destroyed. I figured nobody would think to go in there, so that's where I went, only it was too much street light from fires and lanterns, so I found my way to the cellar and crawled back as far into a dark corner as I could. I told myself I just needed to lie down there for an hour. I just needed to rest. If I could just rest for a while, I'd be better. My wounds — I told myself they weren't too serious. Why, look — how could they be if I'd been able to make it all the way back from the battlefield? So just an hour hidden there and I'd be better. Better enough to go back out and find Frankie. That's what I convinced myself of anyway. And so that's what I did."

I looked around to see if anyone on Caroline Street had taken any notice of us standing there. The Dog and Suds was already closed for the night, so Mrs. Strentz wasn't around, though Uncle Dex was still standing behind the counter inside the Kitchen Sink. He saw me, and waved, but then went back to whatever he was doing. A few people passed us on the sidewalk, but once again, like when we met up with Sally at Federal Hill, we probably just looked to them like four kids with bikes, hanging out and talking. No ghost — or at least no ghost *they* could see or hear.

"I don't remember anything after that," Sally said. "I only remember going inside, like I said." She took a step closer to the building. Then she said, "Like this."

And with another step forward Sally passed through the locked front door and inside the Dog and Suds, vanishing into the darkness, leaving us behind.

·   ·   ·

We all stood there for a good ten minutes after Sally disappeared, feeling empty and lost and helpless.

Greg finally broke the silence.

"Hey, Anderson, your uncle knows all about the history of Fredericksburg. Do you think he'd know when this building was built? Or when it was rebuilt — like, after the war?"

I gave him a quizzical look, wondering why that would matter.

"This is the last thing Sally remembers," he said. "Which must mean this was where she died. What if that's what happened, way down in the cellar or wherever — some place nobody thought to look? What if they tore down the building after the war, not knowing she was in there? Or what if the building collapsed on her? That would explain why she disappeared, why they never found her body, and why she's been stuck here all these years, waiting for, well, I guess, waiting for us to solve the mystery!"

CHAPTER 25

Amazingly, Uncle Dex con-firmed it. "Oh yeah," he said when we asked about the history of the building. Since we'd already had conversations with him about the dogs next door, and about Mrs. Strentz's ghost, and the connection to the Battle of Fredericksburg, it didn't seem like too strange a thing for us to bring up.

"These two buildings share a wall, and they both came down during the battle," he said. He dragged out a photo history of the Civil War and showed us a copy of an old picture of downtown Fredericksburg.

"See that big pile of rubble, with a couple of walls still standing?" he asked. "That was all that was left of these two buildings after the shelling and the looting and the battle. The Union army stayed around for another day in Fredericksburg, withdrawing men who'd been trapped on the battlefield once they finally were able to negotiate a truce. General Burnside decided he'd had enough, after the debacle at Slaughter Pen Farm, and the awful slaughter at Sunken Road. The Army of the Potomac did more damage to the town before they left, not wanting to leave much behind for the Confederates and the citizens of Fredericksburg, just about all of whom — unless they were slaves — supported the Confederacy. There are probably soldiers still buried in places all around Fredericksburg, in unmarked graves, even untraceable graves. Or Confederate and Union soldiers both buried under the rubble of these fallen buildings. In a lot of instances they just built right back over the old foundations, not even bothering to clear everything away."

That sounded creepy — bodies left all over — but with so many casualties, it made sense that they wouldn't always have time to do right by the dead.

So it must have been what Greg said: Sally had died alone and been buried in the basement or cellar of what was now the Dog and Suds building, and never found. Until, sort of, now.

We thanked Uncle Dex. It was almost six o'clock, past time for us all to be home.

Something else occurred to me as we were walking out the door, though, and I turned to ask Uncle Dex one more question.

"I know you've studied a lot about the Battle of Fredericksburg and the history of the town and all," I said. "And I was wondering if you ever came across the name Frank or Frankie Keegan?"

Uncle Dex gave me a funny look, and I thought for a second he was going to ask me why I wanted to know. He just smiled, though, and said, "Well, actually, yes. There was a Dr. Frank Keegan who moved here about ten years after the war. He'd fought in Fredericksburg on the Union side as a member of the Irish Brigade, then he stayed for several weeks working in the hospital across the river at Chatham Manor, helping with the sick and wounded. As I understand it, he became a doctor after the war, somewhere back up north, but I guess always liked Fredericksburg. Or maybe he had some other reason for wanting to move here and open his practice. But that's what he did. Down on Princess Anne Street. And his son became a doctor here, too. And his grandson. And a great-granddaughter or two. There's still a Dr. Keegan who works over at the hospital —

she's in the emergency room — who's his great-great-great-great granddaughter. I went to high school with her. Or maybe she's his great-great-great granddaughter. Anyway, it was one of those ironic things that happened here. Something good, I guess you could say, coming out of something so terrible."

We rode silently for a few blocks toward Deedee's house on Caroline Street down near the city dock — where Sally and the Irish Brigade had crossed the river back in 1862. I wondered if that might have had something to do with why Deedee could see and hear Sally, but probably there was no way to know something like that.

Deedee broke the silence. "Thanks for riding home with me. It's getting pretty dark. I just wish Sally was here so we could tell her all that stuff we learned about where she ended up. And about how things turned out for her little brother."

Greg responded. "Sometimes ghosts can still hear us talking, even if they can't show themselves to us," he said. "So that might have happened."

Julie was worried, too. "I'd hate it if she missed out on what your uncle told us, Anderson," she added. "It'd be terrible if Sally just suddenly ran out of time for us to solve the mystery."

"We'll just have to wait and see," I said, which didn't sound very helpful. But there was nothing else we could do.

CHAPTER 26

A week passed. We met each afternoon in the basement of the Kitchen Sink for band practice, hoping and praying Sally would show up. Mostly we just sat there, discouraged when she didn't, practicing less and less until we stopped altogether. We couldn't believe the mystery could end here, with us finally knowing the answers, but not able to tell Sally. About the only thing that we felt like doing was talking about the Battle of Fredericksburg — especially about the aftermath.

"Robert E. Lee could have ordered the Confederate troops to attack the Union army as it retreated," Julie said one afternoon, just sort of out of the blue. "But he was afraid they would get slaughtered by the Yankees in that same open field."

"That makes sense," Greg said. Then he added, "Did you know that Abraham Lincoln relieved General Burnside of his command of the Army of the Potomac, because the Battle of Fredericksburg was such a disaster?"

I said I'd read that the Confederates believed the northern lights were a sign from God about the righteousness of their cause.

"Yeah," said Greg, "but the Union soldiers believed it was a sign from God about the righteousness of *their* cause, and a signal that they were supposed to continue the fight to end slavery."

"Well, did either of you know that there was a second Battle of Fredericksburg just five months later?" Julie asked.

Greg and I just looked at each other. How could we not know about this?

"Uh, who won?" Greg asked.

"The Union," Julie said. "It was a smaller battle, but once again they used pontoons to cross the river, and once again they attacked the Confederates at Marye's Heights. But they were able to outflank them that time, which was how they won."

"But they still had two more years of war," Greg lamented.

Julie nodded. "Yes, but the tide of the war was turning. So maybe the northern lights *were* a sign — a good sign — for the North."

"For America," I added.

"Right," Julie said. "For America."

· · ·

We'd promised Julie that we would give busking another try, out on the sidewalk in front of Uncle Dex's store, and a week later we decided to do it. We couldn't stay holed up in the basement forever.

So on the next kind of warm afternoon, we plugged in our extension cords and ran them out of the Kitchen Sink to our amps and keyboards. Julie got us all tuned up, Uncle Dex asked us to please play more than just one or two songs over and over, and then we got started.

We quickly ran through our usual songs, plus a couple of other songs we'd learned from our previous ghosts. Then, without even saying anything, we launched into "The Battle Hymn of the Republic." The first time through we did it really fast and loud, sounding like this punk band Julie liked called The Clash. We went so fast, in fact, that it left us all out of breath.

We were sitting there panting — and not getting any tips from anybody passing by — when Deedee came walking up. We hadn't seen her all week, and before anybody could ask, she offered an explanation. "I was grounded," she said. "My mom usually doesn't care, but then sometimes she notices and gets upset. So that's what happened."

We all muttered our condolences, but she wasn't listening. "Do you think you could play that again, and I could sing?" she asked.

Boy, she really was pushy for a fifth grader. But we said yes anyway — it wasn't as if we were making much money doing things our way — only this time we played it slower. At first Deedee's voice was too faint; I could barely hear her. But then she picked up the volume. She actually knew all the words, the same as Sally, and she actually had a nice voice. What was even better, people walking by started throwing money in Greg's guitar case.

We kept playing and Deedee kept singing, and pretty soon a crowd formed — an actual crowd! Mrs. Strentz came out of the Dog and Suds to listen, and Uncle Dex came out of the Kitchen Sink, too.

And then, wonder of wonders, somebody else showed up as well, hovering at the back of the crowd, mostly invisible, though we could see her clearly enough even if nobody else could.

Sally smiled and waved. She mouthed the words "Thank you." She even blew us a kiss, which was the only girly thing she'd ever done the whole time we knew her.

And then, as the song faded out, Sally faded out, too. We hadn't gotten to talk to her, to tell her what we'd learned, but her showing up like that was enough, because in that moment we knew that she'd managed to hear everything — or enough, anyway — to find her peace at least.

The Battle of Fredericksburg was truly and finally over, and the Ghosts of War had made a whopping $23.60.

We might have even found a new lead singer, too.

AUTHOR'S NOTE

The Civil War is a tragic and unfortunate part of America's history. It was a war fought largely due to a difference of opinion among the states about whether slavery should be legal or not. When Abraham Lincoln won the presidential election in 1860 and declared his intention to end slavery, many of the southern states were outraged. During late 1860 and into 1861, the states of South Carolina, Mississippi, Florida, Alabama, Georgia, Louisiana, Texas, Virginia, Arkansas, Tennessee, and North Carolina each seceded from the nation, forming the Confederate States of America. President Lincoln and the Northern states did not recognize this newly formed government, but that didn't stop the South from electing their own president, Jefferson Davis.

The event that is considered to be the official start of the Civil War happened at Fort Sumter in Charleston Bay, South Carolina, on April 12, 1861. The Confederate army demanded the surrender of Fort Sumter, and when the garrison commander, Major Robert Anderson, refused, the Confederate army opened fire. After thirty-four hours of exchanging fire, the fort finally surrendered. From this moment forward, the United States of America was officially at war. And it was a long and bloody war. By the end of the war, roughly 625,000 men (and a few women) lost their lives in the line of duty.

The First Battle of Fredericksburg, which took place from December 11–13, 1862, was one of the bloodiest of the war. It was also one of the most lopsided defeats for the Union army, wasting what should have been a significant strategic advantage that could have led to an early end to the war. Instead, the Battle of Fredericksburg is viewed by many as one of the greatest blunders in American military history. Union troops, with overwhelming numerical superiority, attacked entrenched Confederate positions just south of the town of Fredericksburg, Virginia, and were tragically slaughtered in wave after wave of young soldiers. One book about the battle, written by historians Chris Mackowski and Kristopher D. White, is even titled *Simply Murder*.

It took almost three additional years before the North was finally able to overcome the South. During that time, President Lincoln passed the Emancipation Proclamation, which declared all slaves in the Southern states to be free. Unfortunately, the Southern states refused to abide by this law. Finally, the tide of war started to turn in the Union army's favor in the spring of 1865, and on August 20, 1865, the war was formally declared over. The Confederate States of America was no more. And now that the South was part of the Union again, all slaves were truly free.

As with the previous Ghosts of War books, much of this story is fiction, including the present-day characters, the mystery, and the ghost and her brother. However, the historical figures and major events in this book are all based on fact. There are many excellent books about the Civil War and the Battle of Fredericksburg for those interested in reading further. Mackowski and White's *Simply Murder*, Donald C.

Pfanz's *War So Terrible: A Popular History of the Battle of Fredericksburg*, and DeAnne Blanton and Lauren M. Cook's *They Fought Like Demons: Women Soldiers in the Civil War* were especially helpful in the research and writing of *Fallen in Fredericksburg*.